Coconut Crème Killer

Book Two in the INNcredibly Sweet Series

By

Summer Prescott

ISBN: 9781530583034

COCONUT CREAM

KILLER

Book One in the INNcredibly Sweet Series

TABLE OF CONTENTS

CHAPTER 1 8

CHAPTER 2 18

CHAPTER 3 25

CHAPTER 4 31

CHAPTER 5 44

CHAPTER 6 50

CHAPTER 7 58

CHAPTER 8 68

CHAPTER 9 76

CHAPTER 10 83

CHAPTER 11 94

CHAPTER 12 101

CHAPTER 13 109

CHAPTER 14 115

CHAPTER 15 127

CHAPTER 16 139

CHAPTER 17 151

CHAPTER 18 162

CHAPTER 1

Petite, blonde owner of *The Beach House Bed and Breakfast*, and *Cupcakes in Paradise*, the bake shop right next door, Melissa Gladstone-Beckett, surveyed her latest tray of cupcakes with a nod of satisfaction. She'd worked hard to perfect a recipe that would be just right for the Spring season. Things in the sleepy beachside town of Calgon, Florida tended to slow down a bit as winter's chill lifted from states further north. Tourists visited year round, but typically things didn't get busy again until wedding season began in late May. Thankfully, their peaceful seaside city was under the radar with the Spring Break crowd.

The slower pace gave Missy more time to experiment with new recipes for her cupcake shop, and to spruce things up at the Inn. She was particularly grateful for this brief respite, because she had not one, but two weddings to plan this year.

Picking up one of the lovely cupcakes in front of her, she bit deeply into it, chewing slowly to analyze the flavors. The creative baker had developed a coconut cream cupcake that was sure to be a hit. She'd added coconut milk to the batter, and filled the snow-white and fluffy cake with thick, luscious, vanilla coconut pudding. There was a generous dollop of coconut cream cheese frosting on each, topped with shaved fresh coconut and drizzled with caramel.

Pleased with what she was tasting, Missy closed her eyes and smiled, still chewing. If customers didn't like the cloud-like cakes, she might just eat them all herself.

"Well, my, my, that's a happy face," a teasing voice snapped Missy out of her coconut-induced bliss.

Echo Willis, her flame-haired, free-spirited, former Californian friend was a few minutes early for their daily coffee and cupcake get-together. The women met several mornings a week, along with Echo's fiancé, Phillip "Kel" Kellerman, a local, but world-renowned, artist, to drink coffee, test new cupcake flavors and catch each other up on local events, relationships and scandals. While Missy and Echo were relative newcomers to Calgon, Kel had been born and raised in the town, consequently knowing everyone. He made it a point to keep his finger on the pulse of the business and social scene, filling in the ladies on the latest gossip with a sober glee.

"Oh my goodness, Echo," Missy breathed, blinking her eyes slowly for emphasis. "You have to try these cupcakes. I made a new recipe, and I think that I could cheerfully live on nothing but them."

Echo chuckled, surveying the tray of delectable-looking cakes. "I can't wait. Which ones are vegan?"

"The ones with an almond on top," her friend pointed. "Did you start the coffee before you came back here?"

"Of course. It should be just about ready," Echo replied, delicately using a one finger and her thumb to take both vegan and regular cupcakes from the tray and put them on a plate to bring to their favorite bistro table in the eating area of *Cupcakes in Paradise.*

The friends sat down across the table from each other, and munched happily for a moment.

"You weren't kidding, these are fabulous," Echo said, wiping a crumb from the corner of her mouth.

"Told you," Missy grinned. "Where's Kel? Is he coming this morning?"

"Nope, he's at the gallery already. There's a collector coming in from somewhere exotic to take a look, so he'll be busy schmoozing today."

"Well, that's definitely something that he's good at. Hey, how's business at the candle store?"

Echo had recently opened an adorable little candle shop in a historic building downtown. The whole concept had come about because she'd wanted to invent candles that were scented like Missy's cupcakes. Once the clever gal had learned how to dip, carve and shape the heavenly scented sculptures, she sold them at the cupcake shop and Inn. The sweet-smelling and pretty candles were such a huge hit with tourists and locals alike, that it wasn't long before she'd saved enough to open up her charming shop.

"Business is booming," Echo's face lit up. "Spencer helped me make up several batches last night because my stock was getting low. He's such a sweetheart – it never ceases to amaze me that some pretty young thing hasn't snapped him up yet."

"Somehow, I don't think that Spencer is ready to be snapped up just yet," Missy smiled fondly.

Spencer Bengal was a young, handsome Marine veteran who served as handyman, driver, bartender and breakfast helper at the Inn, as well as filling in at the cupcake shop and candle store as needed. He'd become like a family member to Missy and her clever and dashing husband, Detective Chas Beckett. The extremely capable young man, who could fix seemingly anything, lived in a basement apartment at the Inn, and made himself available to Missy and Chas whenever they needed him. He was in perfect physical condition, muscular and strong, and with his long, raven hair, wide intelligent eyes and a scattering of tattoos, he turned the heads of ladies, both young and old, everywhere he went.

"Who knows?" Echo shrugged, taking a careful sip of her piping hot coffee. "Maybe he just hasn't met the right girl yet."

Echo and Spencer had become close friends, despite their age difference, she being in her early forties, and him being in his mid-twenties. She'd taught him how to dip and sculpt candles, and he helped her out at the store on occasion, if he wasn't too busy at the Inn.

The object of their conversation came in the door just then, and the women exchanged a knowing smile, with Echo stifling a giggle.

"Hey," the Marine grinned, showing dimples that stopped unmarried women in their tracks. "What did I miss?"

"Apparently nothing yet," Missy grinned, as Echo nearly spit out the sip of coffee she had just taken. "What's a nice boy like you doing in a place like this?" she asked, as a means of seeing what he needed.

"Maggie sent me over to let you know that your guest will be arriving soon. She thought that you might want to be there to meet her," Spencer replied, eyeing the plate of cupcakes on the table.

"Take some," Missy waved her hand in the general direction of the cupcakes. "I think you'll like them."

Maggie was the Innkeeper that Missy and Chas had retained when they bought the Inn several months before. The willowy, white-haired woman ran the Inn with grace and efficiency. It was standard procedure for her to send Spencer over to run the cupcake shop when new guests were arriving, freeing Missy up to greet them.

"Just one guest?" Missy asked, gesturing for Spencer to sit, as he wolfed down his first cupcake.

"Yeah, it's kind of weird, actually. She only needs one room, but she rented out the entire Inn so that she would have some privacy," the Marine replied, popping the last half of a cupcake into his mouth, and chewing it with great relish.

Missy set down her coffee cup and stared at him for a moment.

"Hmm…that is odd…why would she do that?"

Spencer swallowed his giant bite, and gratefully accepted the mug of coffee that Echo had gotten up to get for him.

"Thanks," he gave her his signature grin. "From what Maggie told me, I think she's famous or something, and really needs to rest and get away from the real world," he shrugged.

"Well, she came to the right place. It's a relief to be edging into the slow season around here, finally. Do you know her name?"

The Marine shook his head because his mouth was full, then swallowed and replied. "I didn't ask."

"Okay then, you know the drill – I'll go over and take her some cupcakes, and you hold down the fort until I get back," she directed, pushing her chair back.

Missy dearly loved it when Spencer manned the shop for her. His Marine training kicked in and he cleaned, organized and rearranged everything in sight, and it was always an improvement. She knew that, upon her return, the kitchen would be spotless, the tables, countertops and display cases would be gleaming, and fully stocked, and not one thing would be out of place, even if there was a massive rush of people who stopped in. Leaving her shop to Spencer was definitely placing it in good hands.

COCONUT CREAM KILLER: BOOK ONE IN THE INNCREDIBLY SWEET SERIES

CHAPTER 2

"Hi Maggie," Missy greeted the Innkeeper, who had just finished placing fresh flowers on the entry table in the foyer. "Is she here yet?"

Maggie smiled and looked at her watch. "Not just yet, but I'm expecting her at any moment. There is something that I need to warn you about, though," she said quietly.

Missy's eyes widened. "What is it?"

"This guest has rented out the entire Inn because she's introverted, and has been trying to get away from the hustle and bustle so that she can write, so she let me know that she'd not looking to socialize or be catered to, and that we shouldn't be offended if we almost never see her," the Innkeeper confided.

"Write? Is she an author?"

Maggie nodded and grinned. "Oh you could say that," she said, practically bursting to reveal the news. "It's Izzy Gillmore."

Missy's mouth fell open in surprise. "THE Izzy Gillmore? The horror writer?"

"Yep, that's her," the white-haired woman beamed, taking the platter of cupcakes that her boss had carried over.

"I think I've read everything that she's ever written," Missy gasped. "I can't believe she's going to be staying here in our own little Inn. I just love her books and I have so many questions…" she began, but settled down with a sigh when she saw Maggie's reproving look.

"Which is exactly what she's trying to get away from. Okay, I get it. I'll try my best not to be star-struck, but thanks for the warning, I would've died on the spot if she had just walked in here and I wasn't expecting her."

"I think I see a limo pulling up now," Maggie peered over Missy's shoulder, as the owner smoothed down her hair and took a deep breath, preparing to meet one of her literary heroes. "I'll go out to greet her, and you stay in here and take a deep breath," she teased, patting her boss's arm.

"Good idea," Missy nodded, trying to slow her heartbeat.

The soft-voiced, diminutive auburn-haired young woman was not at all what one would expect a horror writer to look like. She was perhaps a bit older than Spencer, and had a fresh, unassuming air about her that Missy found endearing. Izzy Gillmore had rocketed to fame with the release of her first book, and had turned out nothing but hits ever since. It was rumored that she almost never took time off, and wrote for long hours and sometimes days at a time, only taking breaks occasionally.

"You must be Mrs. Beckett," Izzy shook hands with Missy. "It's so nice to meet you. I'll try to be a good house guest," she promised, her wide hazel eyes sparkling.

"It's good to meet you too. Please, make yourself at home. If there's anything you need, ask anyone, or shoot us a text."

"I will, thank you," she nodded, turning to follow Maggie on a tour of the 1860's mansion that had been lovingly updated in a manner consistent with its history.

"Maggie, should I send Spencer over to help with the luggage?" Missy looked meaningfully at the Innkeeper.

"Actually, Miss Gillmore's driver is bringing it in," the Innkeeper replied, with a barely perceptible shrug.

"Okay, then I'll see you gals later. I'm going to head back to the shop," Missy waved and headed for the door.

"Pleasure meeting you," Izzy called out on her way up the stairs.

"You too," Missy replied, still somewhat in awe of having one of her favorite writers sleeping under her own roof.

**

"You knew who was coming to the Inn all along, didn't you?" Missy accused Spencer with a grin.

As expected, the shop was spotless. The Marine had been in constant motion since Missy left, and not one thing was out of place.

"I thought it would be a fun surprise for you," he shrugged, flashing his killer dimples.

"Well, fortunately Maggie clued me in so that I had some time to prepare myself. Have you ever read any of her books? She's amazing, and she's around your age."

"I've read all of them, actually. She's one of my favorites too," he confided.

"Somehow I knew you were a bookworm," Missy teased.

"Guilty as charged, ma'am," Spencer replied, untying the pastel striped apron that he had donned to protect his clothing while he overhauled the cupcake shop.

"Thanks for taking over here," Missy surveyed her gleaming surroundings. "Everything looks great, as usual," she nodded, pleased.

"No problem," the Marine replied easily. "I'm going to head over to the Inn. I have an unruly lawn chaise that needs to be repaired," he explained, heading for the door.

SUMMER PRESCOTT

CHAPTER 3

Detective Chas Beckett always found the air-conditioned, velvet-draped interior of funeral homes to be somehow soothing, despite his line of work. He'd come to Memorial Mortuary today to try to convince the new owner, Timothy Eckels, to accept a position as Calgon's newest Medical Examiner. The previous M.E. had been fired as a result of having tried to frame the socially awkward mortician for murder. Chas had mentioned the position to Tim immediately following the former M. E.'s arrest, but so far had not received an answer.

The pasty, doughy mortician sat at his desk, reading articles on the internet about forensic procedures, and looked up, a bit startled, when the detective appeared in his office doorway. His assistant, an interesting young woman name

Fiona, was on her lunch break, so Chas had slipped in unnoticed. Tim absently pushed his coke-bottle lensed glasses up his nose with a forefinger, and regarded the detective with mild curiosity.

"Has there been an event?" he asked, sounding eerily hopeful.

Chas smiled. The mortician was odd, to be sure, but he respected his work.

"No. At least, not that I'm aware of, but the day is young," he came into the office.

Tim seemed disappointed by the news. "True," he replied, blinking at the detective.

"I actually dropped by to see if you'd given the Medical Examiner position any thought," Chas said casually, easing into a club chair across the desk from Tim.

"I have, but I still don't know if I'd like to accept it," the mortician answered honestly. "I just took over the mortuary, and Fiona isn't completely trained yet…" he began.

The detective nodded. "I understand, and I appreciate that you've agreed to be the interim M.E., but I'd really like you to seriously consider taking the position. I've never seen anyone as thorough as you when it comes to finding minute details on a corpse. It's impressive."

When Tim merely stared at him, he spoke impulsively.

"Look, you certainly don't have to give me an answer now. Go ahead and chew on the idea a bit, take your time. I'd love for you to come over and have dinner with my wife Missy and I. Would you be available tomorrow night?" Chas invited, making a mental note to bring home flowers tonight to break the news to his darling wife that he'd made plans without talking to her first.

"I…available? Umm…I…" Tim stammered.

His introverted soul recoiled at the idea of a social occasion, and as he struggled, the crafty detective sealed the deal.

"Great, we'll expect you around seven. My wife is an amazing cook, you'll love it. I'll email you the address," he said confidently, standing and sticking out his hand.

Tim shook it, seeming stunned by the way he'd been effectively bulldozed. Since he couldn't come up with a valid excuse, he resigned himself to his fate.

"I'll bring a pie," he murmured, staring at the top of his desk.

"Perfect. See you then," Chas gave a jaunty wave and beat feet out of the mortician's office before the timid little man could change his mind.

**

"Oh, what did you do?" Missy asked with a grin after kissing her husband and thanking him for the beautiful bouquet that he'd brought home.

"What? Am I not allowed to make spontaneous gestures of appreciation to my beloved?" the detective asked, with over-the-top disappointment.

"Yes, you absolutely are," his wife crossed her arms and tapped her foot. "Now, what are you up to, Chas Beckett?" she raised an eyebrow at him.

He threw up his hands in mock-surrender and told her about the plans that he'd made with Timothy Eckels.

"I hope that's okay. I really want him to take the position, and I was hoping that we might be able to sway his thinking a bit with some of your homemade biscuits," Chas took Missy in his arms and kissed the top of her head.

"Who knew that I was marrying such a clever, manipulative man who would shamelessly use me for my cooking skills?" she teased, enjoying his embrace.

"Oh good, so you're on board," the detective grinned wickedly. "What's for dinner?"

"Oh honey, after all this…you're taking me out to dinner."

SUMMER PRESCOTT

CHAPTER 4

Izzy Gillmore reclined in her beach lounger, loving the gentle caress of the ocean breeze, but upset with herself because she'd forgotten to bring a bottle of water with her to the beach. Maggie had insisted that if she needed anything, she just had to text, so, hating to bother the staff, but feeling parched, she picked up her phone and requested a bottle of water. Maggie replied immediately letting her know that she'd send one out.

Not five minutes later, one of the most gorgeous men she'd seen in a very long time came trundling down the beach toward her, carrying a cooler and a duffel bag.

"Miss Gillmore?" the tanned, tattooed and muscle-bound young man asked,

"Um, yes?" was the confused reply.

"Hi, I'm Spencer Bengal. Maggie sent me out here with some supplies for you," he grinned, setting down the cooler and duffel bag as though they were weightless.

"Oh, I'm sorry," the auburn-haired beauty frowned, looking adorable. "There must be some mistake, I only asked for a bottle of water," she looked at the cooler and duffel with dismay.

The Marine chuckled and she nearly fainted, seeing those dimples. "Oh, it's never just a bottle of water with Maggie. She never had any kids, so she adopts every one of our guests and spoils them," he explained.

"I told her that I didn't want to be a bother," Izzy worried.

"Everyone tells her that, and this is how she responds," Spencer lifted the lid on the cooler, revealing three different types of water, fruit juices, soda, both diet and regular, a fruit tray, a cold cuts and cheese platter, and a small plastic box of chocolate strawberries.

"Wow, good thing I didn't ask for coffee," the famous horror author joked.

"It's in the duffel, along with sunscreen in two tropical scents, a new tube of lip balm, a set of coasters for your lounger table, a freshly laundered towel, and a sun hat," was the straight-faced reply.

"How am I going to get all of this back to the Inn?" Izzy was dismayed.

"You're not. Whenever you're done for the day, I'll come collect everything, so you don't have a thing to worry about. Is there anything else that I can get for you?" Spencer asked with a twinkle in his eye.

"I can think of anything else that I could possibly want, but thanks anyway," she shook her head, taking it all in.

"Okay, but if you remember something, just shoot us a text," he dazzled her with another warm smile and headed back to the Inn.

"Spencer?" she called out after him.

He turned around, not the least bit annoyed. "Yep?"

"Are you thirsty or anything? Clearly I have plenty to share," the reclusive young woman smiled, biting her lip in a way that the Marine found...interesting.

"Oh. No, thanks, I'm good. Gotta get back to work," he shrugged, noting that she looked somewhat crestfallen at his reply. "But...I'll probably make a fire down here tonight. You're more than welcome to join me, if you're into toasted marshmallows."

"I adore toasted marshmallows," she breathed. "What time?"

"Sometime after the sun goes down. You'll be able to see the flames from the Inn. I'll have Maggie pack up some s'mores supplies and you can just join me whenever you feel like it," Spencer suggested, his heart beating a bit faster at the idea.

"I'd like that," Izzy nodded. "Thank you."

"The pleasure is all mine," he grinned and turned once more to leave.

"Oh, I doubt that," she said, under her breath, watching him jog back up the beach.

The insistent ringing of her phone jarred the author from her preoccupation with the sweet and devastatingly handsome young man who had just delivered her water, and she picked it up with annoyance.

"Hi Miranda," she answered, working hard to keep the annoyance from her voice.

"No, I haven't finished the manuscript yet. I needed some time to myself, so I'm doing a little traveling and I'll get it turned in by the end of the week. That's still way ahead of my deadline," she reminded the persistent and often persnickety publisher on the other end of the line.

"I realize that it has to go through editing, and it'll have plenty of time, I promise," Izzy closed her eyes, thinking that she should perhaps count to ten.

"No, I haven't developed the plot for the next one yet, that isn't due until a week after I send this one. Don't worry, I'll get it to you on time, I always do. Have you scheduled the book tour yet?" she asked.

She hated having to remind Miranda Banks, publisher extraordinaire to do her job, but sometimes the woman needed some pretty strong prompting.

"Well, that has to be done, or it could hugely negatively impact sales numbers. What about the ad placements that we talked about, are those complete?"

Izzy clenched her jaw and took in a deep breath before replying. Her publisher's time would be much better spent promoting the books rather than trying to micromanage the author, but somehow, she didn't think that it would be prudent to point that out.

"Look, Miranda, I've gotta go…something has come up," she said, quickly pushing the End button on her phone. Something had come up indeed…a precious fluffy white maltipoo and a shining golden retriever.

"Well, aren't you two just beautiful," Izzy cooed, holding out her hands for the sweet-natured canines to sniff.

Melissa Gladstone-Beckett, owner of The Beach House, came trotting up to corral her "girls."

"I'm so sorry, they don't normally just walk up and bother people," Missy apologized, slightly out of breath. "This is Toffee, and this little diva is Bitsy, she said, rubbing their ears with great affection.

"They're so sweet," the author exclaimed, clearly enjoying the doggie love that was being lavished upon her. "Clearly they know a sucker when they see one," she giggled.

"They are love bugs," Missy chuckled. "And they're not minding their manners at the moment. I'm sorry if we disturbed you."

"Not at all. My inner introvert shies away from people, not furry babies," she laughed as Toffee swiped the side of her face with a wet, pink tongue.

"So, *I* should go and leave *them* here?" Missy joked.

"Nope, you're a dog person, so you're okay," Izzy grinned. "Maggie sent out a boat load of refreshments if you or the girls are thirsty or hungry," she gestured to the cooler.

Her hostess nodded with approval. "Maggie loves to spoil our guests. If there's any request that you have, no matter what it is, Maggie can make it happen."

"So I've heard," the author shook her head. "I haven't been here very long, but I must say, your Inn has been just the breath of fresh air that I needed…literally and figuratively," she confessed.

"I've come up with tons of ideas for the ending of my novel, as well as the beginning of the next one. But don't tell my publisher that, she'll make me come home early," Izzy made a face.

"A little demanding, eh?" Missy asked ruefully.

"Oh goodness, yes. You have no idea. If I don't produce a certain word count per week, she starts acting like the sky is falling, but I've never missed a deadline yet," she finished firmly.

"Well, good for you," Missy encouraged, giggling as Bitsy leaped up onto Izzy's lap and curled up in a tiny, white ball.

"If it helps at all, I love your books. After I finish one, it's like agony until the next one comes out," she admitted.

"You read my books? That's great – thank you," Izzy said, looking a bit embarrassed.

"Is something wrong?"

"No, no, not at all, it's just…" the best-selling author searched, ironically, for the right words. "It's just that, this all happened so fast. It still seems so surreal that people actually like what I write," she shrugged. "I love what I do, and honestly, I'd do it even if only three people on earth read what I wrote, but it can be a little overwhelming at times. I've had to teach myself how to take a compliment without blushing like a school girl," she laughed softly.

"Oh, honey, I know the feeling," Missy nodded. "I hadn't really dated much at all when I met Chas, and the first time he told me that he thought that I was beautiful, I couldn't form a coherent sentence to save my life. I stammered and kind of gasped, and turned bright red before I could even squeak out a thank you," she chuckled, remembering. "I loved his compliment, but it threw me totally off guard, and since I was shy, it sent all of the blood in my body straight to my face."

"Yes, that's exactly it," Izzy agreed. "The first time that someone asked me to sign one of my books, my hand shook so hard that it looked like a kindergartener had written my name, and it took me forever to process enough words in my mind to put something halfway coherent down on the page."

"Well, don't fret, darlin, I've found that it gets much easier with practice," Missy gave the author a smile.

"Good to know," Izzy replied with a sigh. "You don't sound like you're from around here...I'm going to guess...Texas?"

"Close. I was born and raised in LaChance, Louisiana."

"Well, you have a lovely southern accent. Seriously, I could listen all day."

"Careful what you ask for, hoeny," Missy warned, teasing.

"I love Cajun food, I haven't had any in forever," the author mused.

"Well, I happen to know the breakfast chef, and I'm fairly confident that I can probably talk her into preparing a Cajun breakfast tomorrow, if you'd like."

"Oh my, that would be fantastic," Izzy breathed.

"No problem, sugar. Ask and you'll receive," Missy replied, snapping the leashes onto the dog's collars to let them know that it was time to go.

"Yeah, I'm picking up on that," the young author remarked. "Thanks for letting me get some gratuitous doggie snuggles," she grinned, patting her new canine friends on the head before they had to leave.

"Anytime. Enjoy your day."

"You too."

Missy had only been gone for a matter of moments when Izzy's phone buzzed yet again. Picking it up and seeing Miranda's number, she clicked the button on top to send the call to voicemail, laid back in her lounger, and closed her eyes. The phone rang again, click. And again, click. Once again, and Izzy finally turned the infernal thing off, tired of dealing with it. She took a deep breath of fragrant, salty air, opened a shiny cardboard container of coconut water and drank gratefully, determined to rest and relax, no matter how hard her publisher tried to thwart her effort.

COCONUT CREAM KILLER: BOOK ONE IN THE INNCREDIBLY SWEET SERIES

CHAPTER 5

Spencer Bengal heard Izzy approaching long before she got near the tidy little fire pit that he had built on the beach. He was sitting on a blanket next to the pit, and patted a spot next to him, inviting her to sit.

"Hi," she said, looking uncomfortable. She sat about three feet away from him, on the far edge of the blanket.

"Hi. Beautiful night," he observed, enjoying the cool night air.

"I'm not good at this," she blurted, wrapping her arms around her midsection, as though she were cold.

"Toasting marshmallows? No worries, I have this age-old technique that I can teach you. Works every time," Spencer replied easily, poking at the fire with a stick.

"No, I don't mean the marshmallows. I mean I'm not good at being…human. Like, interacting with other people and not seeming like this huge awkward dork," she confessed miserably, hugging her knees to her chest and staring into the flames.

"That's part of the reason that I wanted to be on this vacation alone. I'm always afraid that I'm going to do or say the wrong thing."

"Well, you seem pretty normal to me, and I've seen some freaky stuff, so…." he smiled at her encouragingly.

"I just…I live my life in my own head a lot, you know? Some people understand that, some people don't. I hate it when people think I'm weird, or crazy," Izzy sighed.

"I think everybody is a little weird and crazy, why should you be the exception?" Spencer teased, and was rewarded with a faint smile.

"Don't worry about what people think. You're talented, you're successful, and it's up to you to decide whether you're happy or not, so just decide that you are, and anybody who doesn't like it can just deal with it," the Marine shrugged.

"Wow, there is seriously more to you than rock-hard abs and a pretty face," Izzy said, then clapped a hand over her mouth as Spencer burst into laughter.

"See? That's what I mean. I just say what I'm thinking, and sometimes forget my filters and make a fool of myself," she shook her head, her face glowing from more than firelight.

"I don't know what you're upset about, I took it as a compliment," he said kindly, still chuckling.

"Who are you anyway?" Izzy asked, catching his eyes, dancing with flames, and holding his gaze.

"I'm just the handyman, bartender, chauffeur, go-fer," he gave her a lopsided grin.

"Uh-huh, and I'm the ghost of Christmas past," she rolled her eyes, feeling more comfortable by the minute with this intriguing young man.

"Pleasure to meet you. Can ghosts eat marshmallows?"

"I'm quite sure that they can," Izzy grinned at last.

Spencer taught her his marshmallow toasting technique and she executed the maneuver expertly, again and again, until they were stuffed.

"There's a story behind those big blue eyes," she mused, looking at him with speculation after they'd flopped back on the blanket to gaze at the stars.

"One or two maybe," was the careful reply.

"Have you ever written about them?" Izzy probed gently.

"I used to write poetry. Haven't for a while."

"Were you any good?"

"I have no idea. I wasn't trying to be good at it, there were just some thoughts and feelings that needed to come out and that seemed like a harmless outlet for that."

"So, why don't you write anymore?"

"Haven't needed to. Life is good."

"Hmm…there must be something to that. I do some of my best writing when life is difficult too."

"Well, you have an advantage," Spencer mused.

"Oh, what's that?"

"If you have an issue with someone, you can just make them die a fictional death," he grinned. "The rest of us just have to put up with stuff."

"There is that," she agreed with a soft laugh.

COCONUT CREAM KILLER: BOOK ONE IN THE INNCREDIBLY SWEET SERIES

CHAPTER 6

Spencer and Izzy stayed lying on the blanket, looking at the stars and chatting like old friends for quite some time, until at last the diminutive author shivered.

"Cold?" the Marine asked.

"A little," she replied ruefully.

She insisted upon helping pack up the marshmallows and other supplies, and after much cajoling, Spencer allowed her to carry the blanket back to the Inn, while he shouldered everything else. The had just stepped into the back yard from the beach when they heard a sharp, splintering sound and saw a flash of bright light from the front yard. There was a screech of tires, and Spencer dropped the load that he was carrying, and sprinted to the front of the Inn, cautioning Izzy to stay put.

There was no way in the world that she wasn't going to go see what had happened, so she put the blanket on top of the pile that Spencer had left, and chased after him, her flip-flops snip-snapping as she ran. When she reached the front of the Inn, she was puzzled. There was a fire burning in the driveway, and Spencer ran toward it with a flowing garden hose, spraying at the blaze before he even stopped running. In no time at all, he had it out, and Izzy was right behind him as he went to examine the cause of it.

"Stay back," he cautioned, holding his arm out to the side. "There's broken glass, I don't want you to get hurt."

"Broken glass?" Izzy's eyes grew wide.

"Yeah, it looks like someone lit up a liquor bottle and threw it," Spencer replied, sweeping the beam of a flashlight that he'd pulled out of his pocket over the shards of glass.

"Let me guess…it was a "Dixie Gentleman" whiskey bottle, wasn't it?" she asked dully.

The Marine whirled around, looking at her closely. "How did you know that?"

"There have been a bunch of weird things happening everywhere I go, and they're all scenes from my books. I thought I'd be safe here," she sighed, her shoulders slumped.

"You need to talk to the police about this," Spencer said quietly. "Let's go up to the house."

"I don't want to bother Missy's husband with any of my issues," Izzy protested.

"Well, he needs to know about a situation that may affect the well-being of a guest, and he also needs to know that someone just committed an act of vandalism on his property," he directed gently.

"So, I have to?" she sighed.

"Fraid so," the Marine nodded. "But don't worry, if he's not at home, we'll just have a regular patrol unit come over and take your statement," he assured her. "And besides, when we go inside, we can get some hot tea to wash down all of those marshmallows."

They needn't have worried about going inside to find Chas, the detective was out on a case. The moment they turned to walk to the front of the Inn, Missy came sprinting down the steps.

"Spencer, what happened?" she demanded, assessing the Marine and his guest to make certain that no one had been hurt.

"This might be a long story," Spencer replied. "If you'd like to take Miss Gillmore inside to get started, I'll take care of things out here and give the police a call."

"Shouldn't we just text Chas?" Missy asked.

"We can, but this is just a case of vandalism, probably some kids messing around."

The worried woman nodded, and led Izzy inside, while Spencer photographed and cleared the crime scene, finding two tire marks where the vehicle that had thrown the Molotov cocktail had peeled out.

**

"So tell me how you're certain that the things that have been happening to you are related to your books," the policeman encouraged Izzy when she had her hands wrapped firmly around a mug of Missy's honeyed tea.

When she heard what had happened to the author, Missy had wisely brought Bitsy and Toffee down to the family room in the Owner's Wing of the Inn, and currently, Bitsy was in Izzy's lap and Toffee was snoozing on her feet. She had left Officer Jenkins to his questioning, knowing that the dogs would help relax the stressed-out young woman. Spencer had come in to join the officer after taking care of the crime scene and putting away the marshmallows and supplies from their evening.

"Every detail is exactly the same as the scenarios in my books. When I went to a book signing in Tennessee, someone left a blue enameled pen that matched the description of a pen in one of my books, and when the local police examined it, they found that it had a capsule of poison in it, just like it was described in the book," she said miserably.

"And there are at least a dozen incidents similar to that, which are all clearly taken right out of my books. None of them have been directly harmful, but they all seem vaguely threatening, particularly if you take their context in the books into consideration," Izzy sighed and put down her mug of tea, scratching Bitsy gently between the ears.

"So, it's a fan," Spencer mused.

"I would hope that a fan would have a more appropriate way of getting my attention. Why would someone who liked my books do these scary things?" she challenged.

"Because people have funny ways of trying to get someone's attention at times," Jenkins speculated. "But he seems to be right in saying that they'd almost have to be a fan to know your books so well."

"It's just so frustrating. All I want is to be left alone," Izzy shook her head and took a sip of tea.

"Maybe that's the problem," Spencer commented.

"What do you mean?"

"Maybe someone wants your attention and they're not getting it," he guessed.

"Don't worry about it, Miss Gillmore. I'll be looking into this for you, and hopefully we can figure something out."

"I'm really sorry about all of this, Officer. I had hoped that whoever was doing this wouldn't find me here, but apparently they're going to find me no matter where I go," Izzy sighed, feeling hopeless and vulnerable.

"I got some tire prints from whoever it was, after they peeled out in front of the driveway, so maybe we can at least identify the tires, and the car," Spencer reassured her.

"My guess is a light blue 1975 Road Ripper pickup truck," she replied staring into space.

"Is that from a book?"

She nodded slowly. "And if it was, you don't even want to know what happens next."

COCONUT CREAM KILLER: BOOK ONE IN THE INNCREDIBLY SWEET SERIES

CHAPTER 7

Missy took a deep breath before heading to the main foyer of the Inn to greet the guest who had just arrived. When she shut the door of the Owner's Wing behind her, the dumpy little man holding a Key Lime pie turned to stare at her from behind coke-bottle glasses.

"Mr. Eckels, how nice to see you again," she greeted him sweetly, extending her hand.

Much to her surprise, he put the pie into it, and continued gazing around the foyer.

"Hi," he said, seeming distracted.

This evening might be even more challenging to get through than Missy had originally thought.

"Chas and I are so glad that you could make it tonight, won't you join me in the dining room?" she invited, taking small steps in that direction and hoping that he would follow.

"Okay," Tim agreed and meandered along behind her.

Once inside the formal dining room of the Inn, Missy placed the delicious-looking Key Lime pie on one end of the table and was ecstatic when Chas appeared in the doorway.

"Tim, glad you could make it," he greeted the mortician warmly, shaking his hand.

"Okay," Tim said, nodding. He seemed a bit overwhelmed by his surroundings and the presence of people.

"I'm starving," the detective greeted his wife with a kiss.

"Well, why don't you boys take a seat, and we'll get started," Missy suggested, hoping that conversation would flow more naturally once the food had been served.

As if on cue, once everyone was seated, Spencer came through the large mahogany door with a tray bearing a soup tureen. His eyes flashed briefly when he saw Tim, and his jaw tightened imperceptibly, but he said nothing as he moved around the table, ladling a luscious lobster bisque into the delicate china bowls in front of Missy, Chas and their guest. After a long look at the mortician that Chas and Missy missed, Spencer returned to the kitchen with the tureen.

"So, how are you liking Calgon, Mr. Eckels?" Missy asked pleasantly, stirring her soup with a spoon.

"Well, I've really only had a chance to see dead bodies so far," he answered honestly, blinking at his hostess.

"Oh!" Missy was startled when she realized that he wasn't kidding. "Well, Echo and I really had a great time helping your assistant with her makeover," she tried again.

Tim's assistant, Fiona, had demanded that he hire her after she met him when her sister was murdered, and he told her that she'd have to remove her multiple piercings and adopt a look that wouldn't scare the families of the deceased if she wanted to work at the mortuary. Desperate to move up in the world, the unique young woman had gone shopping and to various salons with Missy and Echo, coming out looking like a respectable young lady. Now if he could only work on her bossiness a bit.

"She looks different now," he nodded, slurping a spoonful of soup, then dabbing at his lips with a linen napkin.

"So how's business?" Missy asked, ready to kick her husband under the table if he didn't contribute to the conversation at some point.

"Pretty dead," was the deadpan response from Tim.

A hysterical giggle burst forth from Missy and she covered it with her hand, not knowing if her guest would see the humor in his reply.

"Sounds like you might need some supplemental work then," Chas finally broke in. "Being a Medical Examiner would fill that void," he smiled triumphantly, as Missy breathed an inward sigh of relief.

She went to work on the bisque while the men talked business.

"I suppose I have to examine the bodies anyway," Tim mumbled, slurping his soup again and dribbling just a bit onto the napkin in his lap.

"I've seen how you work, Eckels, and I'm really impressed. You found things that the former M.E. missed, on several occasions. I think you'd be a perfect fit for the job, and I can bring in an instructor from Miami to train you for a few weeks until he certifies that you're ready to take charge," the detective offered, in a low key voice, pretending to be terribly interested in his soup, but watching Tim like a hawk for any sort of reaction.

"I'd still be able to prepare the deceased at the mortuary, right?" he asked, blinking at Chas.

"Of course."

"Because you should see some of the hack jobs that are out there prepping the deceased. Eye glue doesn't stick and the eyeball caps pop out when the seam gives way, broken bones poking through skin, causing seepage, there's just no excuse for that kind of shoddy craftsmanship," Tim shook his head in disgust as Missy choked on her soup and ran from the room with a quiet "excuse me."

Spencer was on instant alert when Missy charged into the kitchen and bent over the sink for a moment, taking deep breaths and thinking of kittens, flowers and unicorns. Her stomach rolled uncertainly, and she shook just a little bit.

"What happened out there?" the Marine growled, ready to dart into the dining room.

Missy started to giggle, softly at first, then hysterically, tears streaming from her eyes, as Maggie and Spencer stared at her. Maggie handed her a glass of water, and after taking a couple of sips and calming down a bit, Missy related the dinner conversation.

Maggie clamped her lips together, trying not to laugh, and Spencer glowered fiercely.

"That is one messed up dude," he said in a low voice, his eyes on the door.

"Oh, honey, I think he's just lacking in social skills. I was a fish out of water in there. I threw him every conversational softball that I could think of, and it just didn't go anywhere, but start talking about the dead, and he has plenty to say," she hiccupped as a threat of the giggles struck again.

"Is it safe to go back out there again?" Maggie was grinning from ear to ear.

Missy dabbed at her eyes. "I think so, I'm just glad that we're not serving prime rib," she giggled.

"Or sushi," Maggie added with a snicker, as Spencer shook his head.

The rest of the dinner passed without incident, with Tim and Chas talking about cold cases and destruction of evidence issues. Missy ate quickly and excused herself as soon as was polite, leaving the two men to their gruesome conversation, and taking a slice of gloriously silky Key Lime pie toward the Owner's Wing. Before she got to her private entrance near the bottom of the stairs, she ran into Izzy Gillmore, looking white as a ghost.

"Izzy, honey, what's wrong?" Missy asked, alarmed.

"Who is that man in the dining room?" she whispered, stealing glances in that direction.

"His name is Timothy Eckels. He's the local mortician, why?"

"I know him. He's sent me some strange fan mail in the past, and somehow found out my phone number when I lived in New York."

Missy frowned, concerned.

"Strange? What do you mean?" she asked, keeping her voice low.

"He reads my books and apparently makes notes of the forensic mistakes that I make, and sends them to me," Izzy explained.

"Well, sounds like he's just an attentive fan."

"When he called me in New York, he sounded really offended by the fact that I hadn't done my research. I had mentioned something about the way that bodies were prepared, because it was relevant to a zombie thriller that I'd been writing, and he was all bent out of shape because he felt that I was dispensing misinformation. It didn't help when I told him that most readers wouldn't know the difference or care," she sighed.

"I think I know which book you're talking about," Missy said excitedly. "Is it the one where the doctor travels to the mountains and gets bit by something in a cave, and…" she began, wide-eyed.

"Yes, that's the one," Izzy interrupted, before her hostess got too carried away. "But he used to send me comments on all of them."

"When was the last time he did that?"

"It's hard to say, because he's not the only one who does it, but I think it's been a while," she shrugged, taking nervous glances toward the dining room.

"Well, maybe now that he's made a new start here in Calgon, he doesn't have time to dedicate to correcting your forensic procedure," Missy smiled reassuringly.

"Let's hope so," Izzy nodded, wrapping her arms around her midsection.

COCONUT CREAM KILLER: BOOK ONE IN THE INNCREDIBLY SWEET SERIES

CHAPTER 8

Missy was shaking like a leaf when Izzy came down the stairs and into the dining room for breakfast.

"Are you okay?" the young woman asked, her eyes darting around the room.

"Oh honey," Missy replied shakily. "I'm fine, but whatever you do, don't go outside," she instructed, her eyes wide.

Izzy noticed that the drapes had been drawn in every room and sighed.

"Let me guess…snakes in the trees?" she asked, shaking her head in disgust.

Missy took an involuntary step backward and her mouth dropped open in shock. Her mouth opened and closed like a fish on a bank a couple of times before she could form a coherent sentence.

"Wha…how…how did you know that?" she stammered, looking at the author like she was an alien life form.

"I didn't, I guessed, because that's what happened in the book after the zombie one," Izzy sighed. "But, if they're true to the story, there's no need to worry, the snakes will all be harmless."

"Why did the person in the book do it?" Missy asked, not really wanting to hear the answer.

"Because the heroine in the book was deathly afraid of them, and he was trying to send a message."

Missy shuddered. "That's awful."

Spencer came into the doorway of the dining room, with leaves and debris in his hair and small scratches all over his hands and arms.

"Well, the good news is that it looks like they're all non-venomous," he announced.

"Oh darlin!" Missy exclaimed, clamping her hand over her nose. "I don't mean to be rude, but you…" she looked desperately for something tactful to say.

"Smell?" he supplied for her, making a face. "Yeah, I know. It's a scent that some of the snakes give off when you handle them. The guys from Animal Control have been helping me catch them, but it's like shoveling waves out there."

Missy blanched and worked hard to keep from gagging.

"I'll come out and help, since this is my fault," Izzy muttered, embarrassed.

"Oh, honey, I don't think that you want to…" Missy began, wide-eyed.

Izzy shrugged with resignation. "It's okay. Just because my main character was afraid of snakes doesn't mean that I am. They're just like any other critter. Poor things are probably so confused right about now."

Missy was speechless, and Spencer grinned with approval.

"Yeah, it's unfortunate," he agreed, sobering. "Most of the snakes that were put into the trees weren't tree snakes to begin with. A lot of them fell, some didn't make it," the Marine said soberly.

"Well then, let's go help the ones that did," Izzy replied, determined.

Missy watched them go, feeling slightly embarrassed at being so afraid of the slithery creatures. Toffee chose that moment to brush against her leg, and she nearly jumped out of her skin. Laughing at herself, she bent down to give the silky retriever a hug, and Bitsy came bounding over to join them, tiny ears flopping.

Echo came into the dining room just then.

"Hey girl, there you are! I didn't see you at the cupcake shop and I wondered if something was wrong," Echo came over and hugged her friend, then joined her in giving affection to the "girls."

"Did you know there was a snake on your front porch?" she asked.

Missy went still and stared at her.

"It was just a harmless, little bitty thing, so I picked it up and put it in the grass. Come to think of it, I should probably wash my hands," she said, heading for the kitchen, with Missy trailing along behind her.

"There are tons of snakes in the yard," she murmured with a grimace, then explained what had happened.

"Oh, I can't wait to tell Kel about this," she grinned, knowing how much her fiancé loved a good mystery.

"This is bad though, who knows what will happen next?" Missy worried.

"Well, Izzy does, apparently. The events come straight from her books, and if whoever is doing this, is doing it systematically, then the next event should come right from the following book," Echo replied logically.

"That makes sense, but there's a problem."

"What's that?"

"I haven't read the next book yet," Missy shrugged.

"Looks like we have our afternoon planned for us then, doesn't it? I'll grab a copy of it from the bookstore and take it to the candle shop with me, you download the eBook and read it on your tablet, and we can make notes about the awful things that happen. That way we can narrow down which events are likely to take place."

"Good think we read quickly," Missy bit her lip. "If we know what might happen, we might be able to prevent it."

"Or let it happen and catch the person," Echo looked at her shrewdly.

"I'll talk to Izzy about it too," Missy nodded.

"I'll fill Kel in on what's going on, and we can compare notes tomorrow over coffee and cupcakes. Sound good?"

"Sounds perfect."

Echo wandered over to one of the heavy damask drapes and pulled it aside a bit to observe the snake cleanup in the back yard.

"Well, it looks like those two are getting along well," she turned around and waggled her eyebrows at her friend.

"I'm definitely not coming over there to look," Missy crossed her arms and stayed put.

"They're showing each other the snakes that they've picked up," she narrated. "Now, they're laughing…ooooh, she just put her hand on his arm," she continued.

"Oh, stop it," Missy chuckled. "They have a mutual affection for squirmy, disgusting animals, that's all there is to it, Nosy Nellie," she teased.

"I guess we'll just have to see," Echo replied knowingly, closing the curtain. "Normally I'd stay to watch more of the "Dating Game" in the back yard, but I have a book to buy, so I'm going to run."

"Alright, darlin, I'll see you tomorrow," Missy gave her friend a hug and walked her to the door, keeping her eyes on the porch as Echo stepped out, making certain that nothing squiggled its way inside the house.

There was a distinct possibility that she'd have nightmares tonight, and Missy vowed that she'd let Spencer take the "girls" on their walk for a couple of days…just to be sure that there were no remaining reptiles about.

COCONUT CREAM KILLER: BOOK ONE IN THE INNCREDIBLY SWEET SERIES

CHAPTER 9

Fiona McCamish, Mortuary Assistant, was thrilled at the news that her boss, Timothy Eckels, had accepted at least an interim position as Medical Examiner for Calgon County.

"Does that mean you're going to finally let me do some of the body prep?" she challenged, a gleam in her eye.

Tim blinked at her and sighed.

"No. I've explained this. Preparation of the deceased is an art form that takes years of practice to perfect. I will continue to create art, and you will assist and observe and deal with clients."

"How am I ever going to learn if you never let me do anything?" Fiona complained, hands on hips, tapping her foot impatiently and pushing her lower lip out into a pout.

The hole from the piercing she'd had there was nearly entirely closed, and it was hard to imagine that the attractive young woman had once sported black, shabby clothing, a mohawk and multiple piercings. She'd been attractive before her Missy and Echo makeover, but in a much edgier way.

Tim stared at her. On the one hand, he was annoyed that she was constantly underfoot, asking questions, peering over his shoulder, crowding him as he created his masterpieces, but, at the same time, he found in her a kindred spirit who viewed the preparation of the dead with the proper reverence. It wasn't about the person that the deceased had once been – that person had vacated the vessel – it was about causing the lifeless flesh beneath his hands to resemble the vital person that they had been while still drawing breath. This is what touched the hearts of those left behind, and this was the challenge that prompted the reticent mortician to rise from his bed every morning.

Sighing deeply, Tim frowned at his eager and mildly belligerent young assistant.

"If I allow you to practice on the closed casket remains, will you stop bothering me?" he asked, blinking at her from behind his thick glasses.

"For a while," she grinned, thinking of the challenge that it would be to piece together the remains from accidents of all kinds.

"Fine. When we get a CC in, you can practice, but if your work isn't pristine, you won't even get those," the mortician warned.

He took his business very seriously, and would not allow a hack to attempt to work their craft in his mortuary.

"You got it boss man," Fiona grinned.

Her eyes lit up as she heard the office phone ring, and she dashed from Tim's office to go answer it. Tim didn't answer the phone. To say that he was not a people person was an extreme understatement, so he allowed Fiona to take charge of almost every instance of human contact, be it on the phone or in person. She reappeared in his office a few minutes later.

"That was "Detective Tall-Dark-and-Handsome." You've got a body to investigate," Fiona announced, handing him a yellow sticky note with the address on it.

Tim looked at the sticky note and nodded.

"If I'm late getting back, just lock up at the usual time," he said absently, heading downstairs for his bag. His official training was supposed to start next week, but in the meantime, he knew enough about what he was doing to determine what testing would be necessary to determine criminal activity.

"Remember what you said…if it's an accident…" Fiona called after her boss, who, as usual, declined to reply.

**

Chas greeted Tim Eckels when the mortician arrived at the scene and ducked under the yellow tape that cordoned off the area. The pale, doughy man glanced around the area behind the popular nightclub with distaste. The alley smelled of old beer and older garbage, and he didn't even want to know what went on behind the various stacks of crates and bins.

The detective beckoned Tim to follow him to where a body lay between two industrial-sized dumpsters. What he saw when he got there stopped him in his tracks. The tiny, fit, young woman's beautiful auburn hair splayed out, covering her face as she lay on her stomach.

"Well, there's no doubt that this is a murder," the mortician muttered, noting the pool of blood that had seeped from the victim.

He took a camera that Chas had issued to him upon taking the interim M.E. position, and snapped several photos, making certain that the body wasn't disturbed at all. Once he finished, they turned her over and repeated the process, and then it was time to get to the meat of his task.

**

Spencer Bengal was a man who knew when it was time to reach outside of himself and bring in more resources. Now was such a time. He drove the long familiar road until it turned from asphalt to dirt, eventually withering away into the tangle of Florida swampland. The going was slow, as he made his way to the cabin that had been of such good use to him in the past. He'd last seen his fellow Marine, Janssen, in New York. Missy and Chas had gone on vacation, and Spencer had joined them. He had a job to do, no matter what the locale, and somehow, Janssen had known exactly where to go and how to get there, turning up just in time to do what was necessary.

The man who'd been so scarred by war that he'd been unable to cope with living in the midst of humanity, always seemed to turn up in the nick of time whenever his Marine buddy, Spencer, needed him. Spencer was hoping against hope that that would be the case this time as well, there was a lot on the line, and it would most likely take both of them to do what needed to be done.

He approached the cabin and found the door ajar. Moving slowly, he kept his back to the wall and peered into the windows, seeing a dark figure sitting inside.

"Been a long time, man," Janssen called out. "I hope you brought beer."

Spencer chuckled, held up the six pack in his hand, then jogged to the porch and mounted the steps.

SUMMER PRESCOTT

CHAPTER 10

Missy, Echo and Kel sat down at their favorite bistro table in the eating area of *Cupcakes in Paradise*, determined to puzzle out which awful event that Izzy Gillmore's stalker would be likely to perpetrate next. Echo had brought her brand-new-yet-dog-eared copy of the next book in the series, with passages highlighted, and marked with sticky notes for easy reference.

As usual, when she was upset about something – and after yesterday's reptilian event, she had definitely been a bit upset – Missy had spent some serious kitchen time, and had come up with yet another new cupcake for the trio to try while they dissected Izzy's book for clues. She'd created a dark chocolate cherry masterpiece, using carob for Echo's vegan version, by whipping together cherry pie filling with cream cheese for the creamy center of the cupcake, and topping the luscious dessert off with a generous dollop of fluffy fudge frosting, dark chocolate chips and a juicy cherry. When Kel saw her latest creations, he helped himself to two, despite his resolve to maintain a healthier eating regimen.

"Your cupcakes will surely be the death of me someday, dear lady," he proclaimed, taking a huge bite, being careful to not allow even a single delightful crumb to drop back onto his wrapper.

"Well, we've all gotta go sometime, and all things considered, this way isn't all that bad," Echo teased, swiping her finger through the whipped carob frosting on her vegan cupcake. Missy had even found soy-based cream cheese, so her friend could indulge in nearly the same recipe.

"Hopefully we can figure out Izzy's stalker's next move so that the poor girl doesn't have to face her own mortality anytime soon," Missy said gravely, reminding them why they were all there.

"Indeed," Kel nodded, always one to try to get to the heart of solving a mystery. "In each of her books, there seems to be a pattern involving four non-lethal incidents, and of course, one final, lethal incident," he began, getting down to the business at hand.

The artist had a keen and analytical mind, along with an uncanny insight into people that made him a valuable asset in trying to figure out what might happen next.

"The good news is, the protagonist in her books usually manages to stay a few steps ahead of whatever evil person or force is pursuing them. It's always a secondary character who gets killed, and usually it's done to simply send a message to the main character," he continued.

"So far," Echo interjected.

"What do you mean?" Missy asked, taking a sip of her piping hot coffee.

"The main character has escaped harm so far. That doesn't mean that she hasn't written a book that came after the one that we just read, where the main character is the person who dies. Maybe whoever is doing this is working their way through Izzy's novels, stalking her and scaring her, to lead up to the moment when they actually kill her," she proposed.

Missy shuddered. "Well, I certainly hope not, but if that is the case, then we definitely need to get this figured out and put a stop to it before whoever is doing this goes too far and someone actually gets hurt."

"Where is Izzy this morning? Is she worried at all?" Kel asked, pen poised over his notepad.

"When I came through the Inn, she hadn't come down for breakfast I didn't see her, so I…" Missy stopped speaking abruptly when a tall, willowy blond came in the door of the shop.

"Hello, can I help you?" Missy asked pleasantly, despite the fact that the shop didn't technically open for another hour.

"I hope so," the 30-something woman with a faint East Coast accent replied brightly.

She approached the table with a smile as Kel looked at her pensively.

"I'm sorry, have we met?" he asked, before the woman could continue. "You look so familiar."

She blushed slightly and giggled. "I don't know that we've met, but you may be familiar with my work. I'm Genevieve Lightman, but please, call me Gen," she stuck out her hand and Kel shook it, light dawning in his eyes.

"Genevieve Lightman…the paranormal writer!" he exclaimed. "That's why you look familiar, I recognize you from the back of your books," the artist shook her hand with a smile.

"Oh my goodness, how nice to meet you," Missy introduced herself after Kel had made introductions for himself and Echo. "What brings you to my humble little cupcake shop?" she grinned.

"Well, I originally went over to the Inn, because a little birdie told me that my very dear friend Izzy was staying there. I needed some time off, and figured that if she found an oasis of peace and quiet, I could come down here and surprise her, then relax and unwind for a few days. Your sweet little Innkeeper told me that she hadn't seen Izzy yet this morning, but that I was welcome to walk over to the cupcake shop and see if you knew where she might be, so here I am," Gen finished with a grin.

"And I have to tell you, the combined scent of coffee and cupcakes is just killing me right now," she giggled.

"Well, I don't think that Izzy has made it down to breakfast just yet, but you can go take a look at the cupcake selection and choose whichever ones you'd like to try. I'll run and get you a cup of coffee. We're technically not open yet, but you're welcome to make yourself comfortable and enjoy a coffee and cupcake breakfast with us," Missy offered.

"You are just as sweet as this little shop, and I adore your southern accent, by the way, but actually, if I could get those to-go, I'd love to go sit on the beach."

"Of course, no problem darlin, you just choose your cupcakes and I'll grab a to-go cup of coffee for you. Creams and sugars are on the counter over there, so help yourself."

Gen chose a Coconut Cream cupcake and a Strawberry Lemonade cupcake to go, and was surprised when Missy refused to take any money.

"No, sweetie. Any friend of Izzy's is a friend of ours," Missy waved her off with a smile.

"Thank you so much. When I meet folks like you, I wonder why I don't just move down here to the Sunshine State," she beamed. "It was such a pleasure," the internationally famous "ghost book" author waved to Echo and Kel on her way out, leaving them open-mouthed in her wake.

The three of them sat, staring at the door where Gen had just exited, and finally Echo broke the silence.

"Wow, how many famous authors are we going to meet this week?" she joked.

"What a delightful young lady," Kel nodded. "I've read a few of her books, but I do prefer other authors."

"I haven't read any of her books, but I've seen interviews with her, and she seems just as lovely in person as she is on TV. Apparently, she does a lot of charity work," Missy added. "Now, back to figuring out the stalker's next move..." she said pointedly, tapping her note pad with her pen.

"Okay, the four events to watch out for in this book are…" Echo flipped the pages of her book to reveal the first set of sticky notes. "Blood wiped on the doorjambs of the main character's house…" she began.

"It was goat's blood, wasn't it?" Kel asked, pen poised.

"Yes, because it was a ritualistic thing," Missy nodded. "If the stalker does that, we may be able to figure out who he is by watching the security camera footage," she pointed out. "And no one but the poor, innocent goat will get hurt."

"Second…her bed was set on fire," Echo raised her eyebrows.

"Not a worry. Security is tight enough around here that that could never happen," Missy was relieved.

"Third…a plague of spiders invaded her house."

Kel shuddered visibly and made a face.

"And fourth, she drove out to that remote area by the shipping docks, and when she came back, her tires were slashed and the inside of her car was filled with rotted meat," Echo nearly gagged as she said it.

"Well, if we keep Izzy away from the docks, I think we'll be okay," Kel quipped. "I haven't read this one in a while, remind me of how the victim is killed."

"She goes to a club, and receives an anonymous text that says her ex-boyfriend needs help and is in the alley behind the club. Once she goes outside, the madman grabs her from behind and slashes her throat, then leaves her between two dumpsters," Missy grimaced.

"How do you read all of these grim stories?" Echo shook her head in wonder.

"Because they're not grim. I mean, yes, terrible things happen, but the main character always manages to figure out what to do to save themselves, or humanity, or whatever," she shrugged.

"They're quite well-written too," Kel pointed out.

"True. Izzy does tell a good story. I had to lock all of my doors and windows last night it creeped me out so badly," Echo admitted.

"You mean you haven't been doing that already?" Kel arched an eyebrow at her.

"Well, fortunately, unlike Izzy's characters, I don't seem to run into monsters and serial killers on a regular basis," she rolled her eyes.

"It only takes one," her over-protective fiancé muttered.

"So basically, it looks like we can just alert Spencer to be on the lookout for strangers lurking about after dark, and let the security cameras do their job," Missy shrugged, looking dissatisfied.

"Why do I have the sneaking suspicion that that all sounds just a bit too easy?" Echo murmured.

COCONUT CREAM KILLER: BOOK ONE IN THE INNCREDIBLY SWEET SERIES

CHAPTER 11

Missy closed up the shop and headed to the Inn to see if Maggie needed anything before she took Toffee and Bitsy for their evening walk. The weary owner was shocked to her foundations to hear voices raised in conflict when she opened the door to the grand foyer. Rushing in to see what was happening, she saw a bone-thin woman, with the tanned leathery skin that was typical of many of the retirees that she encountered, and a shock of short red hair, that, in the light of the waning sun, seemed to be aflame. The overly made-up scarecrow of a woman was clearly invading poor, sweet Maggie's personal space, her chin jutting forward as she thrust her face quite near the innkeeper, but the dear woman stood her ground in the face of abject belligerence.

"I'm sorry Ms. Banks, but the privacy of our guests is paramount..." Maggie began, reasonably, and the fiery old crone cut her off.

"Don't you dare speak to me about policy. I know for a fact that Izzy Gillmore is here, she's been using her credit cards, so don't even try me," Ms. Banks threatened, her nasal New York accent thick.

"That girl has been avoiding my calls and she's coming up on a deadline. Now either you tell me where she is or I'll bust down every door in this place until I find her," the woman continued, clearly hopping mad.

Missy had to take a deep breath and really channel her inner southern hostess charm in order to face this dragon of a woman. No one treated Maggie like this, not under Missy's roof.

"Excuse me, is there a problem here?" she asked pleasantly, pasting on a smile, while Maggie remained ramrod straight, staring the rude New Yorker down.

"You're darn tootin' there's a problem here," the woman turned on Missy like a snake ready to strike. "This employee," she jabbed a gnarled finger with an impossibly bright red enameled nail on it in Maggie's direction. "Refuses to give me the simple bit of assistance that I need," she accused, eyes slitted.

"Well, I'd be happy to see what I can do for you," Missy ignored the jab at Maggie, because if she dwelt on it, things might get rather ugly.

"I'm Melissa Gladstone-Beckett, the owner of The Beach House," Missy extended her hand, daring the old prune to ignore it.

She received a perfunctory press from the arthritic grip. "Miranda Banks. It's about time I got to speak to somebody in charge," she huffed, giving Maggie a dirty glare.

"Actually, when it comes to anything related to the Inn, Maggie is in charge," Missy replied with a tight smile. "Maggie, could you go see what Spencer is up to?" she asked innocently.

The Innkeeper gave her a knowing glance and nodded. With a final look of disdain thrown in Miranda Banks' direction, she turned and left the room.

"What seems to be the issue, Ms. Banks?" Missy asked, once Maggie had gone.

"The issue is that one of my writers is holing up here, hiding from me. She isn't answering my calls or emails, and she's coming up on a deadline, so it's imperative that I speak with her," the publisher insisted, her breath smelling of stale cigarette smoke and far too much coffee.

Missy stared at the woman for a moment, now fully understanding why Izzy had been so anxious to be left alone. If this was what she had to deal with on a daily basis, the need for escape was entirely evident.

"I'm sorry, Ms. Banks, but I can't help you," she began.

"Oh yes you can, dearie, and you will. I know that Izzy Gillmore is staying here, and you're going to get her for me right now, or I'm going to go find her myself," she threatened at top volume, leaning in to invade Missy's personal space the way that she had with Maggie. She clearly had no idea who she was dealing with. The southern spitfire drew herself up to her full height and raised an eyebrow at the irate publisher.

"You will do no such thing," Missy said quietly, her kitten-grey eyes burning into the rheumy, faded blue ones in front of her. "I don't know who you think you are, but this is my house and my business that you're barging into and raising your voice like a fishwife. You had no right to treat Maggie unkindly, and you will not order me around like I'm a servant in your home. I've been nice to you up until now, and that's simply because I was raised properly, but you'd better believe you need to turn around and walk out of here right now, before I have you removed."

"First, you had better…" the publisher screeched, before an authoritative male voice cut in, as Spencer seemed to materialize out of thin air.

"Is there a problem here?" he demanded, towering over the now silent harpy.

"You don't intimidate me, young man. You lay one hand on me and I'll slap you with a lawsuit so fast it'll make your head spin," Miranda Banks railed, craning her head to look up at the mountain of a Marine.

"Actually, this young man is my private security guard, and he is absolutely authorized to remove you from this property by whatever means he deems necessary. There's the door, Miranda," Missy's eyes were chips of steel.

The publisher looked from Missy, up to Spencer, and back again.

"You'll regret this," she muttered.

Missy's southern accent was in full twang. "Was that a threat, Ms. Banks?" she challenged, stepping forward to invade the bony woman's space, trying not to breathe in the smell of tobacco and coffee.

"That was a promise," the old crone growled, her crimson slicked lips pulling back to reveal teeth yellowed by age and habits.

Missy never took her eyes off of the publisher.

"Spencer, see Ms. Banks to the door, then escort her from the property. Miranda Banks, if you set foot on these premises again, I'll have you arrested for trespassing, and *that's* a promise," Missy's tone was icy.

SUMMER PRESCOTT

CHAPTER 12

As soon as Spencer went out the door with Miranda Banks and Missy heard the screech of her tires leaving the parking lot, she went to the kitchen to find Maggie.

"Hey darlin, you alright?" she asked, giving the Innkeeper a hug.

"Ooooo! It was so hard to hold my temper with that vile woman," Maggie frowned.

"Oh, tell me about it, honey. I nearly betrayed my genteel upbringing with that one," Missy shook her head.

"Is she gone?" Maggie asked, taking a furtive glance at the kitchen door.

"For now," Spencer replied, walking into the kitchen. "She yelled and threatened all the way to her car, then rolled down the window and kept it up until the car was out of sight."

"That woman is nuts," Maggie commented, an unusual remark out of the woman who made it her mission in life to take care of the needs of others, no matter what their quirks.

"Certifiable," Missy agreed. "I'd better go warn Izzy that she's in town, poor thing," she said, heading for the door.

"Izzy's not here," Spencer stopped her.

Missy's eyes grew wide with concern. "She's not? Where is she?"

"I'm not sure. She told me yesterday that she wanted to explore a bit, so she's probably out doing that," the Marine shrugged.

"We have to find her," Missy breathed. "If the person who is stalking her followed her, she could be in danger."

"Let's not jump to conclusions," Spencer cautioned. "She came here because she wanted to be by herself. Maybe the nicest thing that we can do for her is to let her just disappear for a while."

"But, what if something happens to her?" she worried.

"If the stalker thinks she's here, hiding away in her room, then she shouldn't have anything to worry about, right? If they try anything, our security cameras will pick it up," he replied reasonably.

"I suppose you're right," Missy nodded. "I just worry about the poor little thing."

Missy had given the strange list of things that might happen, based upon what she, Echo and Kel had found in Izzy's book, to Spencer, so that he'd know what he might potentially be dealing with as he kept watch. The fact that the Marine wasn't worried at the moment helped Missy feel better about things, but she was still nervous about when and how the stalker might strike again. Right now, however, she needed to get to her "girls" and take them outside for their walk.

Toffee and Bitsy greeted their human with happy kisses and wagging tails, eager to go for their late afternoon walk on the beach. This was a special time of day for Missy and the "girls," where they enjoyed the warm breezes, sand and surf as the sun started to set. Their routine hardly ever varied, they'd go for a walk to unwind and take care of business, then it was time to head home to make dinner.

Since the beach behind the Inn and cupcake shop was private, Missy and the girls very rarely encountered any people, so she was surprised when she saw a familiar-looking figure sitting on the beach, her feet curled beneath her.

"Hi Genevieve," Missy approached the author, the dogs staying quietly behind her. "You haven't been out here all day, have you?"

"Oh, hi!" The blonde woman looked up with a sunny smile. "No, I haven't been out here all day. When I didn't see Izzy this morning, I went on a tour of Calgon, did some shopping, and came back out here to relax a little bit, thinking I might finally run into that silly girl," she chuckled. "Is it okay that I'm out here?" she asked.

"Oh, of course. It's not a problem at all," Missy assured her. "Where are you staying?"

"Well, actually, I'd been hoping that I might be able to stay with Izzy, but since she seems to have gone into hiding somewhere, I don't know where I'm going to go," Gen shrugged, looking up at Missy and shielding her eyes from the sun with her hand. "Are there any decent hotels nearby?"

Missy thought about the paid-for but not inhabited rooms of the Inn just sitting empty, and made a decision.

"You know what, there's no reason you can't stay here. That way you'll be here when Izzy gets back from wherever she is today. I'll just refund her money for one of the rooms. I'm sure she'll be okay with that once she finds out that it's because you came to surprise her," Missy smiled down at the author.

"Really? Are you sure?"

"Absolutely. Whenever you're done enjoying the sunset, just come on up to the Inn and talk to Maggie, she'll get you set up in a room. Where are your things?"

"Well, I didn't bring much," Gen replied. "I didn't know how long I'd be staying, so everything that I have is under the tree over there by the boardwalk," she pointed to a small suitcase and carry-all a few feet away. Her sandals lay beside her and her toes were dug into the sand.

"Okay, I'll send Spencer down to collect your bags when the girls and I get back to the Inn. He's very sweet and he'll take good care of you," Missy promised.

"Thank you so much. This is going to be such a fun surprise," Gen grinned.

"My pleasure. So, how do you and Izzy know each other?"

"We work for the same publisher, so we've weathered some of the same storms," she smiled wryly.

"I can't even imagine working for that awful woman," Missy shook her head, as Toffee bumped her forehead against the back of her owner's leg, signaling that she was ready to move on. Bitsy made impatient little huffs and chuffs.

"Oh, you've heard some of the stories?"

"No, I experienced her firsthand. She came here looking for Izzy this afternoon – said that she's missing her deadline and she refused to leave. I had to have Spencer escort her from the property," Missy made a face, remembering.

"Oh, wow. I'm sorry that you had to deal with all of that. She's crazy, but you get used to it after a while."

"I don't know that Izzy takes it as well as you do. She was really stressed out when she arrived, and now I can imagine why."

"Yeah, the writing biz isn't for the faint of heart, that's for sure," Gen nodded.

Toffee gave a short woof, indicating highly uncharacteristic impatience.

"Well, it sounds like these girls are ready to get home to their supper, so I'd better get going," Missy apologized. "I'm sure I'll see you soon."

"Looking forward to it," the author waved, and resumed gazing out over the water as Missy and the dogs headed for home.

SUMMER PRESCOTT

CHAPTER 13

Timothy Eckels would have much preferred to have taken the young woman's corpse back to the familiar confines of his own mortuary in order to perform her autopsy, but county policy mandated that the work of exploring the remains for clues be performed at the county morgue, where evidence collected could be quickly catalogued and kept within a proper chain of custody. The county facilities were large and well-equipped, but did not meet the mortician's standards of order and tidiness. He didn't know where anything was kept, and it seemed that whomever had arranged the facility, had no knowledge whatsoever regarding the tools and steps necessary for performing even the most basic functions of the job.

"No wonder Nichimura got fired," the mortician muttered, shaking his head at the stunning incompetence of the former Medical Examiner.

Tim found the tools that he would need for the autopsy, including various evidence containers, and he kept his camera at the ready, so that photos could be taken at different stages of the autopsy process, particularly if something of importance was found. Once the next of kin for this beautiful young redhead could be located, he hoped that the decision would be made to have an open casket, because he relished the thought of being able to turn this cold mound of flesh into a supremely lovely work of art.

It didn't take a rocket scientist, or even a very good forensic practitioner for that matter, to see that the young woman had been murdered. There were bruises on her face, where a hand had been clamped too firmly over her mouth, as the attacker had slashed her throat, killing her almost instantly. The angle of the slice puzzled and intrigued Tim. It looked as though the killer had been shorter than the victim, who was a rather petite woman. The size of the bruises on the face also indicated a smallish hand. Could this young woman's life have been snuffed out by a teenager? Was this a gang related killing? The mortician frowned as he lifted the woman's hair to see if there were any marks on her neck or at the hairline. He did a methodical analysis of the entire corpse, saving the death wound for last, simply because that was typically where the most evidence would be collected. Murder stories were often written and told in the final blow that snuffed a life, at least forensically speaking.

After more than an hour, Tim was finally ready to start examining the neck wound. He had just taken the last photo prior to the exam when Fiona came bursting in the door.

"You started without me," she accused, out of breath.

"I had no intention of starting *with* you," he blinked at her, one gloved hand poised above the death wound.

"Well, I'm never going to be able to learn anything if you don't at least let me watch when you do this stuff," she pointed out, grabbing a protective gown and snapping on latex gloves.

Tim ignored her, and examined the wound, making measurements and speaking his notes into a microphone that was clipped to his gown. Fiona moved to the opposite side of the table from the mortician and acting Medical Examiner, making sure to stay out of his light. Suddenly, he frowned, and leaned closer, far closer than most people would have been able to stomach, to the corpse's neck.

"Do you see that?" he muttered, more to himself than Fiona.

"See what?" she grabbed a magnifying lens from the tray.

"That," he gestured with his forceps at a small white speck within the incision.

Fiona looked at him wide-eyed. "That doesn't look organic," she half-whispered.

"No, it doesn't," Tim frowned more deeply. "Take the camera, and shoot photos where and when I tell you to," he ordered, picking up a scalpel. Carefully peeling layers back, he revealed more of the white object without adding tremendously to the original incision.

"What is it?" Fiona breathed, snapping pictures when ordered to do so.

Tim ignored her question, focusing on his work. He grabbed carefully at the white material with his forceps, and pulled gently.

"That looks like…" Fiona began.

"It is," he cut her off, wanting her to be quiet while he performed the delicate task of extracting the object.

The mortician-turned-medical-examiner got a better grip and tugged until finally the crumpled tubular item slipped free.

"It's like a message in a bottle," Fiona whispered, mystified.

Tim took another pair of forceps and unrolled two pages that had been torn from a paperback book.

"Whoa, dude, what does that mean?" Fiona stared at her boss.

"That means that you go call Detective Beckett," was the grave reply.

SUMMER PRESCOTT

CHAPTER 14

Missy and Chas were enjoying a quiet dinner for two, sitting side by side on the couch and watching a sitcom from the 90's when the detective's work phone buzzed in his pocket.

"Oh no," Missy sighed, putting down her fork.

She'd made a down-home Southern dinner of smoked ribs, barbeque beans, dilled potato salad and hot, fluffy, buttermilk biscuits. The food was delightful, and the company even more so. Missy absolutely loved it when Chas didn't have to work late and they could enjoy a lazy, intimate evening together, snuggled on the couch, with the dogs at their feet.

Chas picked up the call and left the room, while his wife dabbed her biscuit in the sweet rich bean sauce and took a bite. She was still munching when he came back a few minutes later, but put down her plate when she saw the look on his face.

"Bad news?" Missy asked softly, reaching for her husband's hand.

"Strange news," the detective replied, bending down to kiss his beloved. "And unfortunately, it means that I have to go," he sighed.

"It's okay, sweetie, I have a new recipe that I've been wanting to play with lately anyway. You might just come home to a luscious cupcake or two," Missy said playfully.

"All I want to come home to is you, Beautiful," Chas kissed her again and reached for the sport coat that was hung over the back of a chair on his way out.

**

Missy put the leftovers from dinner away, making up a plate in case Chas was hungry when he came home, did the dishes, and took out some notecards so that she could write down recipe notes as she experimented with a new recipe.

She tried several combinations of flavors, and nothing seemed to be working out well, so after a while, she realized that she was too distracted to be creative, and resigned herself to reading in bed. She took the "girls" out one last time, then came in and slipped into her soft cotton pajamas.

Perusing the selection of new books that she'd downloaded over the past few days, Missy settled on an interesting Cozy Mystery about a delicious-sounding deli on Lake Michigan, not feeling ready at all to read anymore horror for a while. She briefly wondered if Izzy had decided to come back to the Inn for the evening, or if she'd found somewhere that she wanted to be for another day, but figured since she hadn't heard anything from Maggie or Spencer, that all was well. The Innkeeper and Marine had gotten Izzy's friend Genevieve settled into a room, and the stately mansion was quiet as everyone settled in for the night.

Missy was only a few chapters into the book, and craving Pastrami sandwiches like crazy, when her eyelids started to droop, and she realized that Chas would once again be coming home to a snoozing wife. Slumber claimed her soon after, her tablet falling to the bed beside her as she drifted off, only to be startled violently awake when a piercing scream ripped through the night.

She immediately grabbed her phone and texted 911 to Spencer, then leaped from the bed, dogs on full alert, grabbing her robe and thrusting her arms through the sleeves as she sprinted for the door to the main Inn. Bursting into the grand foyer, careful not to let the dogs out of the Owner's Wing, she saw Genevieve standing, staring at the front door, pale as a ghost and shaking like a leaf. Following the young woman's gaze, as Spencer came charging in from the kitchen, Missy put her hand over her mouth in shock and horror. There was blood smeared around the entire door frame. It dripped down the sides and formed tiny pools on the pristine white marble below, filling the air with an acrid, coppery scent.

"Goat's blood," she whispered, wrapping her arms around her middle as Genevieve turned to stare at her, eyes vacant.

"What?" the author was confused.

"It's goat's blood," Missy murmured again.

"How do you know that?" Spencer demanded and sprung forward to catch Genevieve as she slipped into a faint.

"Because it's in the book. Take her up to her room please, I'll send Maggie up with tea," Missy directed, texting Chas as fast as her fingers would fly.

**

"I know that this has been a rather disturbing time for you, Miss Lightman," Chas said gently to the pale woman on the couch in her room. "But I need to know what happened, and if you saw anything."

Taking a bracing sip of Maggie's strong tea, Gen nodded.

"I woke up and I was a little bit hungry, and Maggie said that I should help myself to whatever was in the refrigerator whenever I wanted it, so I came down to get a snack, but when I got to the foyer, I smelled something awful, and I looked at the front door…and…" her eyes welled with tears and she swiped at them impatiently.

"And…I saw the…the…"

"The blood?" Chas supplied. Gen nodded.

"Did you notice that there was blood on every doorway in the house?"

The distraught author shook her head.

"I was still kind of half-asleep when I left my room and came down the stairs, but once I saw the front door, I snapped awake. It was so awful."

"Did you see anyone or anything that might be helpful?" the detective probed.

"I don't know," Gen stared into space, trying to remember. "I think I might have seen a shadow go in front of the window, but I don't know if it was just my mind playing tricks on me."

"Why would you think that?"

"Because I was so scared, and because, I don't know, it seemed to be kind of a small shadow for an intruder," she shrugged. "I mean, I write ghost stories for a living, who knows what my mind can conjure up."

"I see," Chas put away his notebook. "Well, I don't know if it's possible at this point, but what you probably need is a good night's rest. Try to get some sleep, and hopefully the morning will shed some light on this whole mess."

"Thank you, Detective," Gen murmured.

"You're more than welcome. If you need anything, just text Spencer or Maggie."

"I will."

The detective followed Maggie out of the room, he'd asked her to be present so that Gen would feel more comfortable, and closed the door behind him, hearing the click of the automatic lock fall into place.

"Hey boss, can I talk to you for a second?" Spencer was waiting for him on the landing.

"Sure, let's go raid the fridge while we talk," Chas replied, as hunger struck with full force. "Maggie, thank you for being in there, I think it made our guest feel much more secure."

"You're welcome. I'm going to turn in, but if there's anything else I can do, just let me know," she replied, turning to head toward her quarters as the gentlemen veered off to the kitchen.

"What's up?" Chas asked, reaching into the refrigerator to grab a platter of deviled eggs, and some thickly sliced honey ham.

"I looked around outside and found this," the Marine held up a plastic baggie containing a cigarette butt with bright red lipstick on it. The front porch area smelled faintly of smoke.

"Any ideas?" the detective examined the contents of the baggie without taking it out.

Spencer told him about the earlier encounter with Miranda Banks, Izzy's publisher, and about the threats that had been made.

"Why didn't you tell me about the incident before?" Chas asked.

The Marine shrugged. "My instincts told me that she was just a nastier than normal old lady. I wouldn't have thought that she was capable of something like this, but, I guess if she was mad enough…" he shook his head, mad at himself for not having been suspicious of Miranda Banks.

"But how would she have gotten inside and back out again?"

"That's what I can't put my finger on," Spencer replied. "I mean, I know she's small, but nothing shows up on the security cameras, there's no sign of forced entry anywhere, no footprints…it's strange."

"What if it's Izzy?" the detective mused.

"Nope," the Marine was adamant. "There's no way. Why would she act out scenes from her own books in someone else's home?"

"Attention?" the detective took a large bite of the succulent ham.

"No way, she's practically a recluse. The last thing that she wants is attention."

"Is she here now? I find it surprising that she wouldn't have heard all of the commotion and come out to see what was going on," Chas raised an eyebrow.

"No one has seen her all day. She may have just skipped town for a bit, to relax and lay low. She never thought that the stalker would find her here. The way that she talked about her publisher, and the way that the crazy old lady acted, I'd believe that she's causing this, one way or another. We just need to catch her in the act."

"And you're positive that it can't be Izzy?"

"Without a doubt, sir. I'd stake my reputation on it," the Marine replied earnestly.

"Then what makes you think that she's okay? She could have been kidnapped."

"All due respect, sir, if the stalker had already grabbed the target, why would he…or she…come back to paint with goat's blood?" Spencer reasoned.

"That's a good point," Chas nodded. He popped a deviled egg in his mouth and chewed with great relish. "It's been a long day."

"Indeed it has," the Marine sighed. "And it'll still be a longer night."

"I appreciate your hard work, Spence," Chas shook his hand.

"It's why I'm here, sir."

SUMMER PRESCOTT

CHAPTER 15

Spencer Bengal sat with his back against the rough-hewn planks of the cabin, the sun steeping him in languorous warmth.

"How's it been?" he asked Janssen, watching him take an appreciative sip of his beer.

"Quiet. Real quiet," the scarred Marine mused, closing his eyes and tilting his face to the sky.

"That a bad thing?" Spencer studied the wild-looking man in front of him.

Janssen lived outside the bounds of society by choice, and it was evident that he spent most of his waking hours in the wilderness, though he was clean and relatively presentable.

"Not this time. I think quiet is okay," he took another long pull on his beer.

"Good. I think the situation is pretty close to being handled, but keep your eyes open," Spencer advised.

"Always do," the Marine mumbled, his face still tilted toward the sun.

"Except now?" his friend chuckled.

"Yup," Janssen grinned.

"What'd you think of the beer?"

"Good. Get something different next time, tho."

"Any special requests?"

"Just something different."

"You got it, brother," Spencer nodded and rose to his feet.

It was so peaceful out, with no sounds but those made by flora and fauna, that he wished he could just stay for a while, but there was apparently a maniac on the loose, and he couldn't afford to take it easy just yet.

**

Detective Chas Beckett shut his office door impatiently. Someone had apparently been brought in for booking, and was caterwauling like a cougar in a carwash. With the lack of sleep that he'd had for the past couple of days, it was difficult to get anything done, and with the racket going on in the station, it was near impossible, so he shut the door and tried his best to ignore it.

The detective had just regained some semblance of concentration when a uniformed officer knocked briefly, then poked his head into Chas's office.

"What is it Briggs?" he sighed, dropping the pen he'd been using onto his desk blotter.

"Sorry to disturb, but there's a woman out here that you need to talk to."

"Is she a dead body, or has she created a dead body?" Chas asked, his voice dripping with sarcasm.

"No sir, but she did ask for you by name, and is leveling some rather disturbing accusations," the cop explained apologetically.

The detective sighed again. Apparently, there was no getting out of this gracefully, he was going to have to go talk to whoever was name-dropping.

"Alright, where is she?"

"Interrogation room three," Briggs replied, ducking out and not bothering to close the door behind him.

Chas heard what sounded like a wheezing Chihuahua yapping loudly and repeatedly, with a heavy New York accent, and debated as to whether or not he should take a couple of ibuprofen now, or after he met with the Chihuahua.

There was a never-ending litany of threats and accusation being brought down upon the poor, unfortunate officer who'd had the extreme misfortune to be in the area of Joe's Bar when the call came in that someone was either drunk and disorderly or disturbing the peace, perhaps both. The tiny little leather-bound woman with candy-apple red hair, who was yammering at the beat cop, paused briefly when Chas came in and took her file from the officer, who vaulted out of his seat like it was on fire.

"Miranda Banks," Chas said, reading the file and thinking what a stroke of luck it was that the woman he'd been wanting to question regarding the vandalism at the Inn was now sitting in his interrogation room.

"You'd better be Detective Beckett, or I swear to all that's holy I'll call your supervisor and the chief of police and my attorney, who'll crawl up the backside of this department with…" Miranda was just warming up when Chas held up a hand, interrupting her.

"I'm Chas Beckett," he said warmly, holding out his hand, which she shook out of sheer surprise at his courtly manner.

"Miranda Banks. These yahoos you've got working in this godforsaken town need a lesson in manners," she said, oozing contempt, but at least doing so a bit more quietly.

"I'm so sorry that you've had a bad experience, Ms. Banks. Are you visiting from out of town?" he asked cordially, sitting down across from her as though she'd invited him over for tea.

"Well, yes, I'm from New York," she replied, eyeing him with suspicion.

"Would you care for a cup of coffee, Ms. Banks? The stuff that they have in the break room is pure pond water, but I could make you a fresh cup in my office," the detective offered, using his big blue eyes to their full advantage.

The cop who'd been standing silently in the corner of the room stared at Beckett as though he'd suddenly sprouted horns.

The old dame narrowed her eyes a bit, but agreed. "It'd be better than being in this dump," she looked around the room with disdain.

"Not by much, but I'll try my best," Chas chuckled.

It was seriously hard work being so charming to the little toad that clip-clopped along behind him in expensive designer kitten heels. He might just have to sit in the hot tub for a while with his lovely wife tonight to wipe this experience from memory.

Miranda sat across the desk from Chas in a soft leather chair, and accepted a cup of delicious Costa Rican coffee, grumbling at the fact that he didn't have artificial sweetener.

"So, are you from the city?" he asked amiably.

"Yep, spent my whole life in Manhattan."

"I'm from upstate," Chas confided.

"I heard of some Becketts upstate, but they were hoity-toity schmucks, so you can't be related," she waved a hand dismissively as the detective covered a smile.

He was indeed one of the hoity-toity Becketts, who had merely chosen a different direction for his life. He had inherited a third of his father's estate, empire, and antique car collection, but chose to stay in police work and attempt to live a normal life.

"So, what brings you to our fair city, Ms. Banks?"

"I'm on vacation," she snapped.

"I see. Are you having a relaxing time?"

"I was until those goons dragged me out of the bar. I was sitting there, minding my own p's and q's and this jerk comes up and asks me how my drink was. He asked me that question, mind you. So, I told him that I didn't particularly care for it, and he offers to get me another one. Why would I want another drink that I didn't like? So I told him that I wasn't gonna pay for the lousy drink and that's when he made a scene. I was just minding my own business," she shrugged, examining her talon-like nails.

"The owner of the bar said that you threatened to grab his private parts and drag him outside for a fight. Does that sound familiar at all?" Chas asked politely.

"That's not how I recall the situation, no," Miranda said primly, gulping at her coffee.

"Okay, well, let me take care of the paperwork on that one. We want to make certain that you enjoy your stay in Florida," he offered, with a conciliatory smile.

"That's the way it should be," she nodded so adamantly that her leathery jowls shook.

"I agree," the detective nodded. "Hey, Miranda...I don't suppose you could help me out a little bit, you know, one New Yorker to another?"

"Maybe. Whaddya need?" her guard went up a tiny bit.

"This bureaucracy just kills me, but...is there any way that I could ask you a few questions, just so that the chief doesn't chew me up on procedure? He's an old school stickler on stuff like that. He doesn't understand how things work where we came from, you know?"

"How long is it gonna take?" the old prune sighed dramatically.

"A cuppa coffee and a New York minute, I swear," Chas raised his hand and put it over his heart, working the blue eyes big time.

"Fine, let's get it over with, but I'll need that refill first," she held out her empty cup.

While he was making the coffee, the detective asked questions casually, friend to friend.

"So, did you hang out at Joe's last night too?"

"Heck no, the place is a dump. I went to the Seaside and had oysters and martinis."

"Goodness, I'm glad you got in safely. You didn't drive did you?"

"Nope, took a cab."

"Do you remember what time it was?"

"Does it matter? Sheesh, what is this Chazzie, an interrogation?" Miranda wheezed a laugh.

"Feels like it, doesn't it?" the detective chuckled. "Confidentially, the chief is all about timelines. He's gotta have a timeline, so if I can just show him that you haven't caused any trouble since you've been here, we're both off the hook."

"Yeah, I hear ya. I'm a hard-core boss sometimes too. I took the cab back to my hotel at around 11:00. Went to the bar at the hotel for a bloody mary – needed my vegetables you know – and then went to bed. Some wild criminal I am, eh?"

"Party girl," he teased, handing her a fresh cup of coffee. "Where are you staying? Nice place on the beach?"

"Nah, I hate sand, it gets in everything, even my teeth," Miranda grimaced and sucked on her teeth. "I'm downtown at the Stafford."

"Nice place. Great prime rib," the detective nodded. "I think I've got enough to pacify the Chief for now, thanks for your patience," he stood.

"You're welcome. I'm a good citizen you know. And if you have any other questions," she looked coquettishly over her shoulder as she headed out the door. "The bar at the Stafford is open until eleven during the week."

"Noted," Chas raised his hand in farewell.

She walked out with one of his worn ceramic coffee mugs in her hand, and he let her go. There were more than enough fingerprints on the arms of the chair and the edge of the desk. There was also the corner from a packet of sugar that had traces of red lipstick on it that looked suspiciously like the lipstick that stained the cigarette butt that Spencer had found outside the Inn. It was fortuitous that Miranda Banks had been busted for disturbing the peace, and it might just lead to a stalking charge against the volatile publisher.

SUMMER PRESCOTT

CHAPTER 16

Chas Beckett took one of Echo's vanilla bean scented candles out of an antique lacquered storage cabinet that was snugged into a discreet corner of his office, setting it on his desk and lighting it after Miranda Banks left, to temper the residual scent of aged cigarette smoke and stale perfume. He wrote down a list of items and poked his head out of the office.

"Briggs," he called out, seeing the officer at the end of the hall.

"Hey, Beckett, man I'm sorry that I had to call you in on that one, but that old bird was losing her mind," Briggs began.

"No worries, it's all good," Chas cut him off. "But if you have a few minutes, there are some things that I need to have chased down."

"I think I owe you that, considering," the officer chuckled. "Whatcha got?"

Chas handed him the list and explained it to him.

"Okay, I need the security footage from the Seaside last night between these times," he pointed to the paper. "Along with the security footage from the Stafford, in the bar and out front, at these times, and call the cab companies to see who made a run from the Seaside to the Stafford within this time frame," the detective ran his forefinger down the list.

"That's it? I'll have this done in a couple of hours," Briggs shrugged. "Don't think I'm strange or anything, but…why does your office smell like cake?" he asked, breathing in deeply.

"It's my candle. I have a friend who makes them. I'll give you her card when you get back," Chas promised with a chuckle.

Having dispatched Briggs to chase down evidence that would either support or disprove Miranda's story, the detective blew out the candle and headed for his car. His next stop would be at the morgue, to go over the strange autopsy results that Timothy Eckels had discovered. Chas felt good about having recommended the rather odd dude for the job. The mortician attacked each case as though determining the cause and circumstances of death was a matter of personal pride to him.

When he arrived at the morgue, he passed Fiona, Tim's equally strange assistant on her way out, power-walking with an air of excited determination.

"Hey Detective," she called out as she steamrolled by.

"Ms. McCamish," Chas replied, amused.

"Timmy is in the office," she called out as she exited the building.

Tim hated when his assistant called him Timmy, which is probably why she did it. Chas just smiled and shook his head. When the detective reached the Medical Examiner's office, Tim was sitting at the desk, oddly, reading a novel.

It was the first time that Chas had seen him reading something other than a technical book or a supply catalog for the mortuary. Timothy Eckels' life revolved around his job, and to see him taking recreational time while at work was entirely unexpected.

When the detective knocked softly on the doorframe to get the utterly absorbed mortician's attention, Tim raised his eyes slowly and blinked several times, clearly still immersed in the world between the pages of the book.

"Your assistant seemed to be in a bit of a hurry."

"There was a terrible car accident, so she'll get to practice her presentation skills. She's on the way to accept delivery of the deceased," the mortician replied without expression.

Chas paused for a moment, staring at the doughy man in front of him. The fascination that he and his assistant had with death was always a bit creepy to him, but he shook off the feeling and got down to business.

"Do you have a moment to talk about the Jane Doe from the other night?"

"I was just researching that," Tim replied, his expression still far away.

"Oh?" Chas was confused. Perhaps the mortician had meant he'd reviewed his notes prior to taking a reading break.

"Yes," he nodded, holding up the novel.

"I'm afraid I don't understand," the detective admitted finally, taking a chair across the desk from the quiet, pasty man behind the coke bottle glasses.

"The papers that I pulled from the wound of the victim came from a book. This book," Tim replied, waggling the novel.

Chas's eyes went to the book with instant laser focus.

"Not this exact book, but this title," the mortician explained hurriedly. "I recognized what was written on the pages because I've read the author's work before, so I thought that maybe the rest of the book might give us a clue as to why the girl was murdered."

"Any ideas?" the detective leaned forward.

"Seems like a ritual. The things that happen to the main character are almost religious in nature. Blood on the doors, plagues of spider's and snakes – maybe this girl was in a cult or something?" the mortician shrugged, then noticed the stunned look on the detective's face. "What?"

"That's hitting a little too close to home," Chas said quietly. "Can you write down the author and title of the book for me?" he asked, his mind racing.

Tim did so, and the detective folded the paper that was handed to him in half and stuck it in his pocket when he stood to go.

"Let me know if you find anything else, I have somewhere that I need to be," he said cryptically, rushing from the room before the mortician could respond.

**

Spencer Bengal knew instantly that something was amiss at the Inn, when he returned from his trip to the cabin and discovered that Missy, Echo, Kel and Maggie were all standing on the front yard, while men dressed in protective gear scurried to and from white panel vans into the Inn.

"What happened?" the Marine jogged over to the group, quickly assessing them to make sure that no one had been hurt.

"Looks like Izzy's stalker struck again," Missy sighed. "I'm really starting to worry about that poor girl. No one has seen her for a couple of days."

"Spiders?" Spencer guessed, based upon what Missy had told him about Izzy's book.

"Yup, they were everywhere," Echo nodded. "It's really cool though, the bug guys have these gently vacuum things that suck up the little guys without hurting them, so that they can be released without being harmed."

"I've heard of that," the Marine nodded. "How many were there?"

"By the time we discovered them, the floor of the Wedgewood parlor was about half an inch deep in them," Missy replied. "We got everybody out, in case any of them were poisonous, and I guess a few of them have been. Gen had already gone out for the morning, so she didn't have to see it."

"They slipped in while I was away," Spencer shook his head. "I should have been here."

"Oh, darlin, don't blame yourself. Whoever is doing this is pretty clever. Scary clever. You can't be expected to be awake and on guard 24/7," Missy patted his thick, tattooed bicep.

"I'm going to go see if they need a hand," he replied, still clearly beating himself up for being gone.

"Be careful," Missy called after him.

"Hey all, what's going on?" Genevieve approached the group from behind, and stood between Echo and Missy, watching the Pest Control specialists scurrying to and fro.

"Oh, it'll be okay, sweetie. We just have a bit of a spider problem, but it'll be taken care of," Missy assured the author.

"Well, thank goodness it's not roaches," Gen shuddered. "I can handle spiders, but roaches creep me out."

"I wouldn't think anything would creep out a paranormal writer," Echo chuckled. "The things that go on in your imagination keep the rest of us up at night."

"The advantage of being the one making up the stories is knowing where they come from. They're not quite as scary when you're the one controlling what happens," the author grinned.

Chas's car pulled into the drive just then, and he jogged over to where the group was standing.

"Spiders?" he asked grimly.

Missy nodded, and he beckoned for her to follow him. Walking quickly over to stand inside the cupcake shop, where he could keep an eye on the Inn and speak privately, the detective regarded his wife gravely. He told her about the clue that had been found in a young woman's death wound, and how Tim had mentioned that there had been incidents in the book that resembled what had been happening at the Inn. The blood drained from Missy's face, and Chas looked at her with concern.

"What did the woman look like?" she whispered.

At her husband's description, Missy swayed a bit.

"Chas, I wish you had met her before she disappeared…I think the victim was Izzy Gillmore. She wrote the book that Tim Eckels was reading."

"I should've questioned her after the first incident. What do you mean "disappeared"?" the detective asked.

"She made it sound like the whole stalking thing wasn't a big deal, but she's been gone for a couple of days now, and…"

"Gone? What do you mean gone? Did she check out?"

"No, she just said that she was going exploring, and she hasn't come back," Missy bit her lip.

"Why didn't you say something, sweetie?" Chas was concerned and a bit hurt.

"Well, she's very reclusive, and had made it clear that she wanted to be left alone, so no one was really sure if she was actually gone or not, and we didn't want to bother her by checking in on her," his wife said miserably.

"And I may have had her killer in my office today," the detective replied grimly. "I'm heading back to the station. Does Spencer know what Izzy Gillmore looks like?"

"Yes, he's talked with her a few times."

"Okay, I'll give him a call if I need an ID on the body."

Chas kissed his wife on the cheek and strode toward his car. He had to find out what Briggs had discovered about Miranda Banks.

SUMMER PRESCOTT

CHAPTER 17

Spencer rejoined Missy, Echo, Kel and Gen, just as Chas pulled out of the parking lot, headed for the police station.

"They can't allow me to help because of safety regulations," he explained, clearly not pleased. "I can't even get near the house."

"That's okay, Spence. We'll just wait for them to finish, then we'll go inside and give the place our own vacuuming," his boss replied, staring into space.

Gen kept fidgeting and bending down to scratch at her ankles.

"Have you encountered poison ivy, dear lady?" Kel asked, gazing down at the welts on her lower legs, some of which were bleeding from having been scratched.

"Oh goodness, I hope not, but it looks like I encountered something," the author was dismayed, looking down at her legs.

"Maybe it's an allergic reaction," Echo suggested, peering down at Gen's ankles.

"Oh dear," she worried, looking helpless.

"I have just the thing," Spencer spoke up. "There's a first aid kit in the cabana with calamine lotion and some antihistamine tablets. Whether it's poison ivy or a simple allergic reaction, between the two, you should be good to go in short order," he explained, his manner subdued. Missy felt bad for the Marine, knowing that he blamed himself for not being at the Inn when the stalker struck again.

"Hey," Echo nudged her best friend after Spencer led Gen to the cabana. "Do you think there's any romantic possibility there?" she speculated, watching the pair walk into the pool area.

Missy raised an eyebrow at her perpetually matchmaking friend. "No, I don't. In fact, I've never seen Spencer so disinterested in an attractive female since I've known him," she mused.

"It's obviously because he's secretly pining for me," Echo batted her eyes as Kel guffawed behind her.

"Yes, I'm sure that's it, sweetie," Missy rolled her eyes.

**

Chas Beckett went immediately to the evidence room at the station and checked out the box of items that had been collected at the murder scene behind the club, looking for one thing in particular, and finding it almost immediately. He picked up the baggie containing a cigarette butt that had the same color of red lipstick as the one found on his front porch, after the goat's blood incident. The DNA results from the butts wouldn't be back for a while yet, but when they came in, he bet that they would match the swab that had been taken from the ceramic mug that Miranda Banks had left at the front counter of the police station on her way out.

"Hey, Detective," Briggs popped his head into Chas's office. "You got a minute?"

"Yes, I do. I was just about to look for you, actually. Have a seat," he offered. "What did you find out?"

"Her story is legit," the officer shrugged, handing over a file folder with a report on what he'd found in the security tapes, and a transcript of his call with the cab company that had transported the leathery diva from the bar to the hotel.

"The times matched up with her story, and the bartenders from the bar and the hotel confirmed that they had had to deal with her," Briggs chuckled.

Chas frowned. Miranda's extensive alibi had checked out on every front, yet there was evidence that looked like it came from her at two different crime scenes. Something wasn't adding up.

**

Spencer had been meticulous in his examination of the welts on Genevieve's legs as he'd put on rubber gloves and carefully coated her with calamine lotion. She took the antihistamine tablet that he offered with a thank you and a smoky look.

"You're really quite good at this…have you had medical training?" she flirted.

"Every Marine learns basic triage skills," he shrugged, peeling off his gloves and helping her to her feet. "Let me help you to your room – it looks like the Pest Control crew is finally gone."

"Well, I'd like that very much. Thank you, Mr…?"

"Spencer, Spencer Bengal."

"Bengal? Like the tiger? Rawr…" Gen growled playfully.

The Marine didn't crack a smile.

"Yeah, like the tiger," he replied, leading the way to the Inn.

The pair went in the back door, through the kitchen, past the dining room, and into the grand foyer, and stopped short, both of them staring.

Genevieve went deathly white, and her mouth dropped open as she stared at her fellow author, Izzy Gillmore.

"You…you're alive, but…how…?" she gasped, looking nauseated, her hands at her throat.

Izzy's eyes flashed and she spoke through her teeth.

"Yes, I'm alive, why wouldn't I be? And what exactly do you think you're doing here? How did you find me?" the tiny auburn-haired author seethed.

Spencer watched the two of them with surprise. Gen had said that she was Izzy's best friend, and Izzy's manner indicated that she was anything but.

"I...oh..." the tall, blonde author slumped into a faint, and Spencer caught her neatly, heading up the stairs toward her room, the set of skeleton keys in his pocket.

"What's wrong with her?" Izzy asked with a disgusted grimace.

"A combination of things, I think. Surprise at seeing you, a heavy dose of antihistamine, and perhaps the bites from several spiders," the Marine guessed nonchalantly.

He climbed the stairs, carrying the passed-out author as though she weighed nothing, then let himself into her room with his passkey, Izzy trailing along in his wake. Placing

Gen on the couch, he texted 911 to Chas, and began searching her room.

By the time the detective arrived, Genevieve was just starting to come around, and Chas had an ambulance attendant evaluate her before placing her in handcuffs and putting her in a patrol car.

"Show me what you've got," he directed Spencer.

"This," he held up a corner of a plastic baggie full of lipstick-covered cigarette butts that had apparently been collected from Miranda Banks' ashtrays and kept so that Gen could plant them at the scene of every act of vandalism that she committed.

"And this," he flipped up the bedspread to show a squirt bottle stained with remnants of goat's blood. "And this," he nudged a nightshirt that was puddled on the floor with his foot, exposing spots of blood on the trim.

"And, most importantly…these," he pointed to a paperback version of Izzy's book that had passages highlighted and underlined, and had two pages which described the murder torn out of it. Next to it lay a large knife that had traces of blood on the handle.

"Good work," the detective shook Spencer's hand.

"It was Gen, the whole time," Izzy murmured, shaking her head. "I knew she hated me, but I never thought that she'd do something like this. I honestly thought that it was either Miranda or the weird mortuary dude."

"It makes sense though, if you know Genevieve's history," Kel chimed in from the doorway, as Chas, Spencer and Izzy turned to look at him.

"How so?" the detective asked.

"Turns out that she gets the inspiration for most of her horror stories from a stint that she spent in an institution that her ultra-wealthy parents put her in when her imagination was a bit much for them to handle. I did some digging because I found it rather suspicious that she happened to show up just when Izzy disappeared, and no trace of a vandal could be found outside the house, even on the security cameras," the artist explained.

"Which meant that the vandal came from inside the house," Chas nodded. "She seemed so frightened and honest that I didn't suspect her," he shook his head, disgusted with himself. He didn't get fooled very often.

"I wonder if she set the fires too," Izzy mumbled.

"Fires?" Chas asked.

"Another author friend of mine had her house burned down. They ruled it arson, but never found the culprit. Gen hated her almost as much as she hated me," she explained quietly.

"Why did she hate you?" Spencer asked, his eyes fixed on the beauty in front of him.

"Because my books were more successful than hers. Miranda always gave me the best tour slots and took all of my calls," Izzy shrugged.

"And where have you been these last few days, dear lady?" Kel asked.

Before she could answer, Spencer interjected.

"She told me that she wanted to get away from it all, so I took her to one of those rental cabins down in the Everglades. Turned out to be a great idea," he finished hurriedly, as Chas eyed him curiously.

"You knew that she was alive and well and didn't say anything," the detective asked mildly.

"Didn't seem prudent at the time, sir," Spencer replied, his eyes locking on Chas's.

Chas nodded.

CHAPTER 18

"I can't believe I invited a stalker and murderer to stay under the same roof where her intended victim was trying to hide out," Missy dropped her chin into her palm and poked at the fluffy frosting of a coconut cream cupcake.

She, Echo and Kel were back to having their morning get-togethers at the cupcake shop now that things had settled down a bit at the Inn.

"You can't blame yourself," Echo patted her friend's hand reassuringly. "We all thought that the stalker was that nasty publisher Miranda."

As if her words had conjured the woman, Miranda Banks threw open the front door of *Cupcakes in Paradise* with sufficient force that the panes of glass rattled.

"Alright, I'm here, where is she?" the aged redhead demanded.

Missy, Echo and Kel stared at her open-mouthed.

"Am I not enunciating well enough for you slow-moving southern folk?" she demanded, jumping a bit when the door opened behind her and Izzy appeared.

"Well, it's about time," she snapped at the young woman, who hugged her anyway. "You're late as usual. Where's the manuscript?"

Izzy strolled over to a table, leading the reluctant publisher by the hand, grinning.

"The manuscript was emailed to you last night, and you know it," she replied, seating herself at a bistro table near Missy's. "I know that you know it, because I could tell that you've opened it and reviewed it already. I've met my deadline, the book is good, and you have nothing left to shout about, so stop posturing in front of these nice folks and have a darn cupcake," the tiny author ordered sweetly, a butterfly in the face of a dragon.

"You're trying to kill me with sugar, aren't you?" Miranda narrowed her eyes, but her tone softened…a bit.

"Die smiling," Izzy batted her eyes at the old woman, finally making her crack a small smile.

"Your incorrigible," the publisher accused.

"And you're impossible," she shot back with a chuckle.

"When are you returning to New York?" Miranda demanded, eyeing the cupcake and coffee that Missy set in front of her with vague suspicion.

"Not for a while," Izzy replied dreamily staring out the window at Spencer, who was planting flowers beside the circular drive. "I kinda like the scenery," she murmured.

"Don't you get distracted young lady. You have deadlines to meet, and the first one that you miss by even a day, I'm going to send henchmen out here to drag you home, you got that?" the publisher shook a bony finger at Izzy, then picked up her cupcake and took a bite, leaving a smear of lipstick in the frosting.

"I've never missed a deadline yet, and I don't intend to start anytime soon," she replied calmly, delicately pulling a piece from her cupcake and popping it in her mouth.

Echo and Kel discreetly hugged Missy and slipped out while the two women chatted more civilly about Izzy's new book, and Missy disappeared into the kitchen to check on a batch of cupcakes that needed to come out of the oven. She hummed to herself as she worked, smiling at the look that she'd seen on Izzy's face when the young woman watched Spencer work. It'd be interesting to see what developed there.

**

Spencer trotted down the steps that led to his basement apartment, not surprised at all to see Janssen sitting in his living room, drinking a craft beer.

"I'm assuming this was for me?" he raised the bottle when Spencer strode in.

"You know it," he nodded and took a seat in a nearby chair.

The apartment was sparsely furnished and everything was symmetrically arranged. The Marine liked it that way – everything he owned had a specific place, and he could tell if anything had been moved even a fraction of an inch. His cat, Moose, so named for his colossal size, jumped up onto his lap and scrutinized Janssen carefully while feigning disinterest and licking his paw.

Spencer looked at Janssen curiously for a moment. "She came back early," he commented, stroking the silky spot between Moose's ears.

"She started walking toward the road," he shrugged. "I couldn't let her see me, so I followed her for a ways, just to make sure she got out of the woods, so to speak. When she got close to the road, I grabbed her from behind, let her know that she was okay, and just made her stay put until a ride came along."

"How'd you manage that?" Spencer sat forward.

"Called in a favor," Janssen replied, leaving it at that.

"You could've warned me."

"Not in time, I had to work with the situation when it presented itself, bro."

"I get that," the Marine nodded.

"She gone now?"

"Nah, planning on hanging out here for a bit," Spencer replied, suddenly fascinated with Moose.

"Uh-huh," Janssen narrowed his eyes. "That wouldn't have anything to do with you, now would it?"

"No way. She's a grown woman, she does what she wants."

The scarred Marine, who lived in the wild because it was safer for him than society, regarded the man across from him with grave concern.

"You can't get involved, man. You know that. First you get too friendly with these people..." he began.

"They're family now," Spencer interrupted the thought, eyes blazing.

"That's what I mean, man. You're too close to them, and now you're getting moony-eyed over some chick. You walking a thin line and you know it," Janssen stared him down.

"There's nothing between me and the writer. And I know what I'm doing with these people – it's part of the job, and it's how I'm choosing to handle it."

"What book did you get that from?" was the quiet reply, as Janssen stood to go. "You know what can happen if you screw up just this much," he placed his thumb and forefinger a short distance apart.

"I won't," Spencer insisted, his jaw muscles flexing.

"Uh-huh," Janssen said again, giving him a long look. "Thanks for the beer, man," he said quietly, and like a ghost, he was gone.

**

Izzy Gillmore thought that she saw a shadow in the trees next to the cupcake shop, but felt no sense of danger as whoever it was continued on their way. She tilted her face to the sun and smiled. She loved the ocean, loved Florida, and loved being out from under the micro-managing eyes of her publisher. Suddenly the future seemed much brighter...almost as bright as a certain pair of blue eyes that she couldn't even begin to get out of her mind.

Made in the USA
Columbia, SC
17 May 2021